WILLIAM SHAKESPEARE:
THE TRAGEDY OF ROMEO AND JULIET

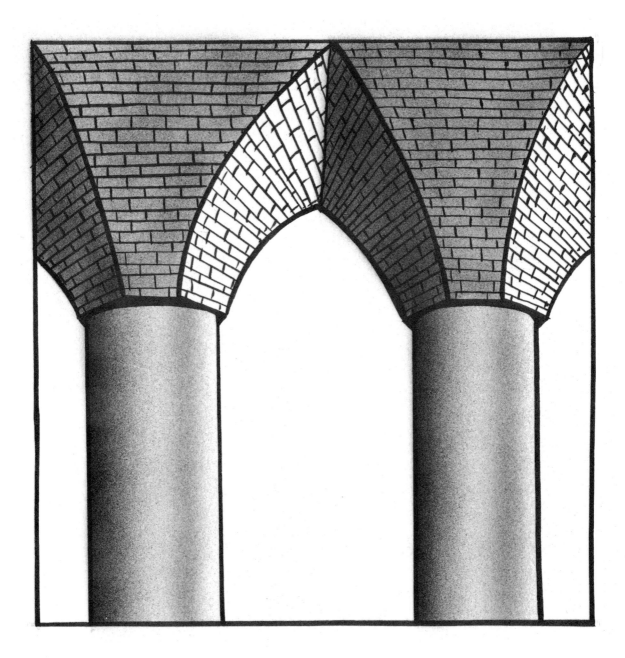

ROMEO AND JULIET

By WILLIAM SHAKESPEARE

DESIGN BY DANIEL HABERMAN
ILLUSTRATIONS BY ISADORE SELTZER

PUBLISHED BY
A. HOROWITZ & SON
RAE PUBLISHING CO., INC.
FINCH, PRUYN & COMPANY, INC.
ROYAL COMPOSING ROOM, INC.

INTRODUCTION—*A star-crossed tragedy*

Romeo and Juliet, by William Shakespeare, is the twelfth in a
series of annual keepsakes prepared for the friends of the publishers.

The Tragedy of Romeo and Juliet was completed in 1595-6; the prolific poet
also wrote a *Midsummer Night's Dream* and *Richard II* between 1594 and 1596.
The first edition of *Romeo and Juliet* in 1597 mentioned a performance by
"Lord Hunsdon's servants"—the name used by Shakespeare's company
until March 1597.

Samuel Coleridge has lectured that "…the main distinction between this play
and others is…that the parts are less happily combined…[yet] grand portions
are produced…the application of judgment and taste…are not to be
attained but by painful study, and to the sacrifice of the stronger pleasures
derived from the dazzling light which a man of genius throws over every
circumstance…taste is an attainment after a poet has been disciplined by
experience.…In my mind it would be a hopeless symptom, as regards genius,
if I found a young man with anything like perfect taste."

The first folio edition of 1623 was used as a guide in the preparation of this
book. The publishers are once again indebted to Isadore Seltzer, whose
illustrations reflect sensitive attention to the characters in the play,
and whose time was generously given.

Scene: Verona and Mantua

PROLOGUE—*Arthur Brooke*
From the Tragicall Historye of Romeus and Iuliet (1562)

TO THE READER:

...And as eche flower yeldeth hony to the bee: so every exaumple ministreth good lessons, to the well disposed mynde. The glorious triumphe of the continent man upon the lustes of wanton fleshe, incourageth men to honest restraynt of wyld affections, the shamefull and wretched endes of such, as have yelded their libertie thrall to fowle desires, teache men to witholde themselves from the hedlong fall of loose dishonestie. So, to lyke effect, by sundry meanes, the good mans exaumple byddeth men to be good, and the evill mans mischefe, warneth men not to be evyll. To this good ende, serve all ill endes, of yll begynnynges.

And to this ende (good Reader) is this tragicall matter written, to describe unto thee a coople of unfortunate lovers, thralling themselves to unhonest desire, neglecting the authoritie and advise of parents and frendes, conferring their principall counsels with dronken gossyppes, and superstitious friers (the naturally fitte instrumentes of unchastitie) attemptyng all adventures of peryll, for thattaynyng of their wished lust, usyng auriculer confession (the kay of whoredome, and treason) for furtheraunce of theyr purpose, abusyng the honorable name of lawefull marriage, to cloke the shame of stolne contractes, finallye, by all meanes of unhonest lyfe, hastyng to most unhappye deathe...

DRAMATIS PERSONAE

ESCALUS, *Prince of Verona*

PARIS, *a young count, kinsman to the Prince*

MONTAGUE, *political rival to Capulet*

CAPULET, *political rival to Montague*

ROMEO, *son to Montague*

MERCUTIO, *kinsman to the Prince and friend to Romeo*

BENVOLIO, *nephew to Montague and friend to Romeo*

TYBALT, *nephew to Lady Capulet*

FRIAR LAWRENCE, FRIAR JOHN, *Franciscans*

LADY MONTAGUE, *wife to Montague*

LADY CAPULET, *wife to Capulet*

JULIET, *daughter to Capulet*

NURSE *to Juliet*

CITIZENS OF VERONA, MASKERS, WATCHMEN, TORCHBEARERS, PAGES, GUARDS, SERVANTS, OTHERS

ACT ONE

MERCUTIO

THE PROLOGUE

[Enter Chorus]

Chorus. Two households, both alike in dignity,
In fair Verona, where we lay our scene,
From ancient grudge break to new mutiny,
Where civil blood makes civil hands unclean.
From forth the fatal loins of these two foes
A pair of star-crossed lovers take their life;
Whose misadventured piteous overthrows
Doth with their death bury their parents' strife.
The fearful passage of their death-marked love,
And the continuance of their parents' rage,
Which, but their children's end, naught could remove,
Is now the two hours' traffic of our stage;
The which if you with patient ears attend,
What here shall miss, our toil shall strive to mend.
[Exit]

SCENE I

VERONA. A PUBLIC PLACE

[Enter Sampson and Gregory, with swords
and bucklers, both of the house of Capulet]

Sampson.   Gregory, on my word, we'll not carry coals.

Gregory.   No, for then we should be colliers.

Sampson.   I mean, and we be in choler, we'll draw.

Gregory.   Ay, while you live, draw your neck out of collar.

Sampson.   I strike quickly, being moved.

Gregory.   But thou art not quickly moved to strike.

Sampson.   A dog of the house of Montague moves me.

Gregory.   To move is to stir, and to be valiant is to stand. Therefore, if thou art moved, thou run'st away.

Sampson.   A dog of that house shall move me to stand. I will take the wall of any man or maid of Montague's.

Gregory.   That shows thee a weak slave; for the weakest goes to the wall.

Sampson. 'Tis true; and therefore women, being the weaker vessels, are ever thrust to the wall. Therefore I will push Montague's men from the wall and thrust his maids to the wall.

Gregory. The quarrel is between our masters and us their men.

Sampson. 'Tis all one. I will show myself a tyrant. When I have fought with the men, I will be civil with the maids—I will cut off their heads.

Gregory. The heads of the maids?

Sampson. Ay, the heads of the maids or their maidenheads. Take it in what sense thou wilt.

Gregory. They must take it in sense that feel it.

Sampson. Me they shall feel while I am able to stand; and 'tis known I am a pretty piece of flesh.

Gregory. 'Tis well thou art not fish; if thou hadst, thou hadst been Poor John. Draw thy tool! Here comes two of the house of Montagues.

   [*Enter two other Servingmen, Abram and Balthasar*]

Sampson. My naked weapon is out. Quarrel! I will back thee.

Gregory. How? Turn thy back and run?

Sampson.	Fear me not.
Gregory.	No, marry. I fear thee!
Sampson.	Let us take the law of our sides; let them begin.
Gregory.	I will frown as I pass by, and let them take it as they list.
Sampson.	Nay, as they dare. I will bite my thumb at them, which is disgrace to them if they bear it.
Abram.	Do you bite your thumb at us, sir?
Sampson.	I do bite my thumb, sir.
Abram.	Do you bite your thumb at us, sir?
Sampson.	[*Aside to Gregory*] Is the law of our side if I say ay?
Gregory.	[*Aside to Sampson*] No.
Sampson.	No, sir, I do not bite my thumb at you, sir; but I bite my thumb, sir.
Gregory.	Do you quarrel, sir?
Abram.	Quarrel, sir? No, sir.
Sampson.	But if you do, sir, I am for you. I serve as good a man as you.
Abram.	No better.
Sampson.	Well, sir.

[*Enter Benvolio*]

Gregory.	Say "better." Here comes one of my master's kinsmen.
Sampson.	Yes, better, sir.
Abram.	You lie.
Sampson.	Draw, if you be men. Gregory, remember thy swashing blow.
	[They fight]
Benvolio.	Part, fools!
	Put up your swords. You know not what you do.
	[Enter Tybalt]
Tybalt.	What, art thou drawn among these heartless hinds?
	Turn thee, Benvolio; look upon thy death.
Benvolio.	I do but keep the peace. Put up thy sword,
	Or manage it to part these men with me.

Tybalt. What, drawn, and talk of peace? I hate the word
As I hate hell, all Montagues, and thee.
Have at thee, coward!

[They fight: Enter an Officer and several Citizens with clubs or partisans]

Officer. Clubs, bills, and partisans! Strike! Beat them
down! Down with the Capulets! Down with the
Montagues!

[Enter old Capulet in his gown, and his Wife]

Capulet. What noise is this? Give me my long sword, ho!

Lady Capulet. A crutch, a crutch! Why call you for a sword?

Capulet. My sword, I say! Old Montague is come
And flourishes his blade in spite of me.

[Enter old Montague and his Wife]

Montague. Thou villain Capulet!—Hold me not; let me go.

Lady Montague. Thou shalt not stir one foot to seek a foe.

[Enter Prince Escalus, with his Train]

Prince. Rebellious subjects, enemies to peace,
Profaners of this neighbor-stainèd steel—
Will they not hear? What, ho! You men, you beasts,
That quench the fire of your pernicious rage
With purple fountains issuing from your veins!
On pain of torture, from those bloody hands
Throw your mistempered weapons to the ground
And hear the sentence of your movèd prince.
Three civil brawls, bred of an airy word
By thee, old Capulet, and Montague,
Have thrice disturbed the quiet of our streets
And made Verona's ancient citizens
Cast by their grave beseeming ornaments
To wield old partisans, in hands as old,
Cank'red with peace, to part your cank'red hate.
If ever you disturb our streets again,
Your lives shall pay the forfeit of the peace.
For this time all the rest depart away.
You, Capulet, shall go along with me;
And, Montague, come you this afternoon,
To know our farther pleasure in this case,
To old Freetown, our common judgment place.
Once more, on pain of death, all men depart.
　　　[*Exeunt all but Montague, his Wife, and Benvolio*]

Montague.	Who set this ancient quarrel new abroach?
	Speak, nephew, were you by when it began?
Benvolio.	Here were the servants of your adversary
	And yours, close fighting ere I did approach.
	I drew to part them. In the instant came
	The fiery Tybalt, with his sword prepared;
	Which, as he breathed defiance to my ears,
	He swung about his head and cut the winds,
	Who, nothing hurt withal, hissed him in scorn.
	While we were interchanging thrusts and blows,
	Came more and more, and fought on part and part,
	Till the Prince came, who parted either part.
Lady Montague.	O, where is Romeo? Saw you him today?
	Right glad I am he was not at this fray.
Benvolio.	Madam, an hour before the worshiped sun
	Peered forth the golden window of the East,
	A troubled mind drave me to walk abroad;
	Where, underneath the grove of sycamore

That westward rooteth from this city side,
So early walking did I see your son.
Towards him I made, but he was ware of me
And stole into the covert of the wood.
I, measuring his affections by my own,
Which then most sought where most might not be found,
Being one too many by my weary self,
Pursued my humor not pursuing his,
And gladly shunned who gladly fled from me.

Montague. Many a morning hath he there been seen,
With tears augmenting the fresh morning's dew,
Adding to clouds more clouds with his deep sighs;
But all so soon as the all-cheering sun
Should in the farthest East begin to draw
The shady curtains from Aurora's bed,
Away from light steals home my heavy son
And private in his chamber pens himself,
Shuts up his windows, locks fair daylight out,
And makes himself an artificial night.
Black and portentous must this humor prove
Unless good counsel may the cause remove.

Benvolio.	My noble uncle, do you know the cause?
Montague.	I neither know it nor can learn of him.
Benvolio.	Have you importuned him by any means?
Montague.	Both by myself and many other friends;
	But he, his own affections' counselor,
	Is to himself—I will not say how true—
	But to himself so secret and so close,
	So far from sounding and discovery,
	As is the bud bit with an envious worm
	Ere he can spread his sweet leaves to the air
	Or dedicate his beauty to the sun.
	Could we but learn from whence his sorrows grow,
	We would as willingly give cure as know.

[*Enter Romeo*]

Benvolio.	See, where he comes. So please you step aside;
	I'll know his grievance, or be much denied.
Montague.	I would thou wert so happy by thy stay
	To hear true shrift. Come, madam, let's away.

[*Exeunt Montague and Wife*]

Benvolio.	Good morrow, cousin.
Romeo.	Is the day so young?
Benvolio.	But new struck nine.

Romeo.	Ay me! Sad hours seem long.
	Was that my father that went hence so fast?
Benvolio.	It was. What sadness lengthens Romeo's hours?
Romeo.	Not having that which having makes them short.
Benvolio.	In love?
Romeo.	Out—
Benvolio.	Of love?
Romeo.	Out of her favor where I am in love.
Benvolio.	Alas that love, so gentle in his view,
	Should be so tyrannous and rough in proof!
Romeo.	Alas that love, whose view is muffled still,
	Should without eyes see pathways to his will!
	Where shall we dine? O me! What fray was here?
	Yet tell me not, for I have heard it all.
	Here's much to do with hate, but more with love.
	Why then, O brawling love, O loving hate,
	O anything, of nothing first created!
	O heavy lightness, serious vanity,
	Misshapen chaos of well-seeming forms,
	Feather of lead, bright smoke, cold fire, sick health,
	Still-waking sleep, that is not what it is!
	This love feel I, that feel no love in this.
	Dost thou not laugh?

Benvolio.	No, coz, I rather weep.
Romeo.	Good heart, at what?
Benvolio.	At thy good heart's oppression.
Romeo.	Why, such is love's transgression.

Griefs of mine own lie heavy in my breast,
Which thou wilt propagate, to have it prest
With more of thine. This love that thou hast shown
Doth add more grief to too much of mine own.
Love is a smoke made with the fume of sighs;
Being purged, a fire sparkling in lovers' eyes;
Being vexed, a sea nourished with loving tears.
What is it else? A madness most discreet,
A choking gall, and a preserving sweet.
Farewell, my coz.

Benvolio. Soft! I will go along.
And if you leave me so, you do me wrong.

Romeo. Tut! I have lost myself; I am not here;
This is not Romeo, he's some other where.

Benvolio. Tell me in sadness, who is that you love?

Romeo. What, shall I groan and tell thee?

Benvolio.	Groan? Why, no;
	But sadly tell me who.
Romeo.	Bid a sick man in sadness make his will.
	Ah, word ill urged to one that is so ill!
	In sadness, cousin, I do love a woman.
Benvolio.	I aimed so near when I supposed you loved.
Romeo.	A right good markman. And she's fair I love.
Benvolio.	A right fair mark, fair coz, is soonest hit.
Romeo.	Well, in that hit you miss. She'll not be hit
	With Cupid's arrow. She hath Dian's wit,
	And, in strong proof of chastity well armed,
	From Love's weak childish bow she lives uncharmed.
	She will not stay the siege of loving terms,
	Nor bide th' encounter of assailing eyes,
	Nor ope her lap to saint-seducing gold.
	O, she is rich in beauty; only poor
	That, when she dies, with beauty dies her store.
Benvolio.	Then she hath sworn that she will still live chaste?

Romeo. She hath, and in that sparing make huge waste;

For beauty, starved with her severity,

Cuts beauty off from all posterity.

She is too fair, too wise, wisely too fair,

To merit bliss by making me despair.

She hath forsworn to love, and in that vow

Do I live dead that live to tell it now.

Benvolio. Be ruled by me; forget to think of her.

Romeo. O, teach me how I should forget to think!

Benvolio. By giving liberty unto thine eyes.

Examine other beauties.

Romeo.   'Tis the way

To call hers, exquisite, in question more.

These happy masks that kiss fair ladies' brows,

Being black puts us in mind they hide the fair.

He that is strucken blind cannot forget

The precious treasure of his eyesight lost.

Show me a mistress that is passing fair:

What doth her beauty serve but as a note

Where I may read who passed that passing fair?

Farewell. Thou canst not teach me to forget.

Benvolio. I'll pay that doctrine, or else die in debt.

[*Exeunt*]

[*Enter Capulet, County Paris,*
with the Clown, his Servant]

Capulet.   But Montague is bound as well as I,

In penalty alike; and 'tis not hard, I think,

For men so old as we to keep the peace.

Paris.   Of honorable reckoning are you both,

And pity 'tis you lived at odds so long.

But now, my lord, what say you to my suit?

Capulet.   But saying o'er what I have said before:

My child is yet a stranger in the world,

She hath not seen the change of fourteen years;

Let two more summers wither in their pride

Ere we may think her ripe to be a bride.

Paris.   Younger than she are happy mothers made.

Capulet.   And too soon marred are those so early made.

Earth hath swallowèd all my hopes but she;

She is the hopeful lady of my earth.

But woo her, gentle Paris, get her heart;

My will to her consent is but a part.

And she agreed, within her scope of choice

Lies my consent and fair according voice.
This night I hold an old accustomed feast,
Whereto I have invited many a guest,
Such as I love; and you among the store,
One more, most welcome, makes my number more.
At my poor house look to behold this night
Earth-treading stars that make dark heaven light.
Such comfort as do lusty young men feel
When well-appareled April on the heel
Of limping Winter treads, even such delight
Among fresh fennel buds shall you this night
Inherit at my house. Hear all, all see,
And like her most whose merit most shall be;
Which, on more view of many, mine, being one,
May stand in number, though in reck'ning none.
Come, go with me. [*To Servant, giving him a paper*]
                Go, sirrah, trudge about
Through fair Verona; find those persons out
Whose names are written there, and to them say
My house and welcome on their pleasure stay.
   [*Exit with Paris*]

Servant. Find them out whose names are written here? It is written that the shoemaker should meddle with his yard and the tailor with his last, the fisher with his pencil and the painter with his nets; but I am sent to find those persons whose names are here writ, and can never find what names the writing person hath here writ. I must to the learned. In good time!

[*Enter Benvolio and Romeo*]

Benvolio. Tut, man, one fire burns out another's burning;
One pain is less'ned by another's anguish;
Turn giddy, and be holp by backward turning;
One desperate grief cures with another's languish.
Take thou some new infection to thy eye,
And the rank poison of the old will die.

Romeo. Your plantain leaf is excellent for that.

Benvolio. For what, I pray thee?

Romeo. For your broken shin.

Benvolio. Why, Romeo, art thou mad?

Romeo. Not mad, but bound more than a madman is;
Shut up in prison, kept without my food,
Whipped and tormented and—God-den, good fellow.

Servant. God gi' go-den. I pray, sir, can you read?

Romeo. Ay, mine own fortune in my misery.

Servant. Perhaps you have learned it without book.
But, I pray, can you read anything you see?

Romeo. Ay, if I know the letters and the language.

Servant. Ye say honestly. Rest you merry.

Romeo. Stay, fellow; I can read.
[*Reads letter*]
"Signior Martino and his wife and daughters;
County Anselm and his beauteous sisters;
The lady widow of Vitruvio;
Signior Placentio and his lovely nieces;
Mercutio and his brother Valentine;
Mine uncle Capulet, his wife and daughters;
My fair niece Rosaline; Livia;
Signior Valentio and his cousin Tybalt;
Lucio and the lively Helena."
A fair assembly. Whither should they come?

Servant.	Up.
Romeo.	Whither? To supper?
Servant.	To our house.
Romeo.	Whose house?
Servant.	My master's.
Romeo.	Indeed I should have asked you that before.
Servant.	Now I'll tell you without asking. My master is the great rich Capulet; and if you be not of the house of Montagues, I pray come and crush a cup of wine. Rest you merry.
	[*Exit*]
Benvolio.	At this same ancient feast of Capulet's Sups the fair Rosaline whom thou so loves; With all the admirèd beauties of Verona. Go thither, and with unattainted eye Compare her face with some that I shall show, And I will make thee think thy swan a crow.

Romeo. When the devout religion of mine eye
Maintains such falsehood, then turn tears to fires;
And these, who, often drowned, could never die,
Transparent heretics, be burnt for liars!
One fairer than my love? The all-seeing sun
Ne'er saw her match since first the world begun.

Benvolio. Tut! you saw her fair, none else being by,
Herself poised with herself in either eye;
But in that crystal scales let there be weighed
Your lady's love against some other maid
That I will show you shining at this feast,
And she shall scant show well that now seems best.

Romeo. I'll go along, no such sight to be shown,
But to rejoice in splendor of mine own.

　　　[Exeunt]

SCENE III

A ROOM IN CAPULET'S HOUSE

[*Enter Capulet's Wife, and Nurse*]

Lady Capulet.   Nurse, where's my daughter? Call her forth to me.

Nurse.   Now, by my maidenhead at twelve year old,
I bade her come. What, lamb! What, ladybird!
God forbid, where's this girl? What, Juliet!

[*Enter Juliet*]

Juliet.   How now? Who calls?

Nurse.   Your mother.

Juliet.   Madam, I am here.
What is your will?

Lady Capulet.   This is the matter—Nurse, give leave awhile;
We must talk in secret. Nurse, come back again.
I have rememb'red me; thou 's hear our counsel.
Thou knowest my daughter's of a pretty age.

Nurse.   Faith, I can tell her age unto an hour.

Lady Capulet.	She's not fourteen.
Nurse.	I'll lay fourteen of my teeth—

And yet, to my teen be it spoken, I have but four—
She's not fourteen. How long is it now
To Lammastide?

Lady Capulet.	A fortnight and odd days.
Nurse.	Even or odd, of all days in the year,

Come Lammas Eve at night shall she be fourteen.
Susan and she (God rest all Christian souls!)
Were of an age. Well, Susan is with God;
She was too good for me. But, as I said,
On Lammas Eve at night shall she be fourteen;
That shall she, marry; I remember it well.
'Tis since the earthquake now eleven years;
And she was weaned (I never shall forget it),
Of all the days of the year, upon that day;
For I had then laid wormwood to my dug,
Sitting in the sun under the dovehouse wall.
My lord and you were then at Mantua.
Nay, I do bear a brain. But, as I said,
When it did taste the wormwood on the nipple
Of my dug and felt it bitter, pretty fool,

BENVOLIO

To see it tetchy and fall out with the dug!
Shake, quoth the dovehouse! 'Twas no need, I trow,
To bid me trudge.
And since that time it is eleven years,
For then she could stand high-lone; nay, by th' rood,
She could have run and waddled all about;
For even the day before, she broke her brow;
And then my husband (God be with his soul!
'A was a merry man) took up the child.
"Yea," quoth he, "dost thou fall upon thy face?
Thou wilt fall backward when thou hast more wit;
Wilt thou not, Jule?" and, by my holidam,
The pretty wretch left crying and said, "Ay."
To see now how a jest shall come about!
I warrant, and I should live a thousand years,
I never should forget it. "Wilt thou not, Jule?" quoth he,
And, pretty fool, it stinted and said, "Ay."

Lady Capulet.   Enough of this. I pray thee hold thy peace.

Nurse.	Yes, madam. Yet I cannot choose but laugh
	To think it should leave crying and say, "Ay."
	And yet, I warrant, it had upon it brow
	A bump as big as a young cock'rel's stone;
	A perilous knock; and it cried bitterly.
	"Yea," quoth my husband, "fall'st upon thy face?
	Thou wilt fall backward when thou comest to age,
	Wilt thou not, Jule?" It stinted and said, "Ay."
Juliet.	And stint thou too, I pray thee, nurse, say I.
Nurse.	Peace, I have done. God mark thee to His grace!
	Thou wast the prettiest babe that e'er I nursed.
	And I might live to see thee married once,
	I have my wish.
Lady Capulet.	Marry, that "marry" is the very theme
	I came to talk of. Tell me, daughter Juliet,
	How stands your dispositions to be married?
Juliet.	It is an honor that I dream not of.
Nurse.	An honor? Were not I thine only nurse,
	I would say thou hadst sucked wisdom from thy teat.

Lady Capulet. Well, think of marriage now. Younger than you,
Here in Verona, ladies of esteem,
Are made already mothers. By my count,
I was your mother much upon these years
That you are now a maid. Thus then in brief:
The valiant Paris seeks you for his love.

Nurse. A man, young lady! Lady, such a man
As all the world—Why, he's a man of wax.

Lady Capulet. Verona's summer hath not such a flower.

Nurse. Nay, he's a flower, in faith—a very flower.

Lady Capulet. What say you? Can you love the gentleman?
This night you shall behold him at our feast.
Read o'er the volume of young Paris' face,
And find delight writ there with beauty's pen;
Examine every married lineament,
And see how one another lends content;
And what obscured in this fair volume lies
Find written in the margent of his eyes.
This precious book of love, this unbound lover,
To beautify him only lacks a cover.
The fish lives in the sea, and 'tis much pride
For fair without the fair within to hide.

That book in many's eyes doth share the glory,
That in gold clasps locks in the golden story;
So shall you share all that he doth possess,
By having him making yourself no less.

Nurse. No less? Nay, bigger! Women grow by men.

Lady Capulet. Speak briefly, can you like of Paris' love?

Juliet. I'll look to like, if looking liking move;
But no more deep will I endart mine eye
Than your consent gives strength to make it fly.

[*Enter Servingman*]

Servingman. Madam, the guests are come, supper served up,
you called, my young lady asked for, the nurse
cursed in the pantry, and everything in extrem-
ity. I must hence to wait. I beseech you follow
straight.

[*Exit*]

Lady Capulet. We follow thee. Juliet, the County stays.

Nurse. Go, girl, seek happy nights to happy days.

[*Exeunt*]

[*Enter Romeo, Mercutio, Benvolio, with*
five or six other Maskers; Torchbearers]

Romeo. What, shall this speech be spoke for our excuse?
Or shall we on without apology?

Benvolio. The date is out of such prolixity.
We'll have no Cupid hoodwinked with a scarf,
Bearing a Tartar's painted bow of lath,
Scaring the ladies like a crowkeeper;
Nor no without-book prologue, faintly spoke
After the prompter, for our entrance;
But, let them measure us by what they will,
We'll measure them a measure and be gone.

Romeo. Give me a torch. I am not for this ambling.
Being but heavy, I will bear the light.

Mercutio. Nay, gentle Romeo, we must have you dance.

Romeo. Not I, believe me. You have dancing shoes
With nimble soles; I have a soul of lead
So stakes me to the ground I cannot move.

Mercutio.	You are a lover. Borrow Cupid's wings
	And soar with them above a common bound.
Romeo.	I am too sore enpiercèd with his shaft
	To soar with his light feathers; and so bound
	I cannot bound a pitch above dull woe.
	Under love's heavy burden do I sink.
Mercutio.	And, to sink in it, should you burden love—
	Too great oppression for a tender thing.
Romeo.	Is love a tender thing? It is too rough,
	Too rude, too boist'rous, and it pricks like thorn.
Mercutio.	If love be rough with you, be rough with love;
	Prick love for pricking, and you beat love down.
	Give me a case to put my visage in.
	A visor for a visor! What care I
	What curious eye doth quote deformities?
	Here are the beetle brows shall blush for me.
Benvolio.	Come, knock and enter; and no sooner in
	But every man betake him to his legs.
Romeo.	A torch for me! Let wantons light of heart
	Tickle the senseless rushes with their heels;
	For I am proverbed with a grandsire phrase,
	I'll be a candleholder and look on;
	The game was ne'er so fair, and I am done.

Mercutio.	Tut! Dun's the mouse, the constable's own word!
	If thou art Dun, we'll draw thee from the mire
	Of this sir-reverence love, wherein thou stickest
	Up to the ears. Come, we burn daylight, ho!
Romeo.	Nay, that's not so.
Mercutio.	I mean, sir, in delay
	We waste our lights in vain, like lights by day.
	Take our good meaning, for our judgment sits
	Five times in that ere once in our five wits.
Romeo.	And we mean well in going to this masque,
	But 'tis no wit to go.
Mercutio.	Why, may one ask?
Romeo.	I dreamt a dream tonight.
Mercutio.	And so did I.
Romeo.	Well, what was yours?
Mercutio.	That dreamers often lie.
Romeo.	In bed asleep, while they do dream things true.

Mercutio. O, then I see Queen Mab hath been with you.

She is the fairies' midwife, and she comes

In shape no bigger than an agate stone

On the forefinger of an alderman,

Drawn with a team of little atomies

Over men's noses as they lie asleep;

Her wagon spokes made of long spinners' legs,

The cover, of the wings of grasshoppers;

Her traces, of the smallest spider web;

Her collars, of the moonshine's wat'ry beams;

Her whip, of cricket's bone; the lash, of film;

Her wagoner, a small gray-coated gnat,

Not half so big as a round little worm

Pricked from the lazy finger of a maid;

Her chariot is an empty hazelnut,

Made by the joiner squirrel or old grub,

Time out o' mind the fairies' coachmakers.

And in this state she gallops night by night

Through lovers' brains, and then they dream of love;

On courtiers' knees, that dream on curtsies straight;

O'er lawyers' fingers, who straight dream on fees;

O'er ladies' lips, who straight on kisses dream,

Which oft the angry Mab with blisters plagues,
Because their breath with sweetmeats tainted are.
Sometime she gallops o'er a courtier's nose,
And then dreams he of smelling out a suit;
And sometime comes she with a tithe pig's tail
Tickling a parson's nose as 'a lies asleep,
Then he dreams of another benefice.
Sometime she driveth o'er a soldier's neck,
And then dreams he of cutting foreign throats,
Of breaches, ambuscadoes, Spanish blades,
Of healths five fathom deep; and then anon
Drums in his ear, at which he starts and wakes,
And being thus frighted, swears a prayer or two
And sleeps again. This is that very Mab
That plats the manes of horses in the night
And bakes the elflocks in foul sluttish hairs,
Which once untangled much misfortune bodes.
This is the hag, when maids lie on their backs,
That presses them and learns them first to bear,
Making them women of good carriage.
This is she—

Romeo.   Peace, peace, Mercutio, peace!
Thou talk'st of nothing.

Mercutio. True, I talk of dreams;
Which are the children of an idle brain,
Begot of nothing but vain fantasy;
Which is as thin of substance as the air,
And more inconstant than the wind, who woos
Even now the frozen bosom of the North
And, being angered, puffs away from thence,
Turning his side to the dew-dropping South.

Benvolio. This wind you talk of blows us from ourselves.
Supper is done, and we shall come too late.

Romeo. I fear, too early; for my mind misgives
Some consequence yet hanging in the stars
Shall bitterly begin his fearful date
With this night's revels and expire the term
Of a despisèd life, closed in my breast,
By some vile forfeit of untimely death.
But he that hath the steerage of my course
Direct my sail! On, lusty gentlemen!

Benvolio. Strike, drum.

[*They march about the stage, and retire to one side*]

SCENE V
A HALL IN CAPULET'S HOUSE

[*Servingmen come forth with napkins*]

First Servingman. Where's Potpan, that he helps not to take away? He shift a trencher! He scrape a trencher!

Second Servingman. When good manners shall lie all in one or two men's hands, and they unwashed too, 'tis a foul thing.

First Servingman. Away with the join-stools, remove the court cupboard, look to the plate. Good thou, save me a piece of marchpane, and, as thou loves me, let the porter let in Susan Grindstone and Nell. Anthony, and Potpan!

Second Servingman. Ay, boy, ready.

First Servingman. You are looked for and called for, asked for and sought for, in the great chamber.

Third Servingman. We cannot be here and there too. Cheerly, boys! Be brisk awhile, and the longer liver take all.
[*Exeunt*]

Capulet.   Welcome, gentlemen! Ladies that have their toes
Unplagued with corns will walk a bout with you.
Ah, my mistresses, which of you all
Will now deny to dance? She that makes dainty,
She I'll swear hath corns. Am I come near ye now?
Welcome, gentlemen! I have seen the day
That I have worn a visor and could tell
A whispering tale in a fair lady's ear,
Such as would please. 'Tis gone, 'tis gone, 'tis gone.
You are welcome, gentlemen! Come, musicians, play.
            [Music plays, and they dance]
A hall, a hall! Give room! And foot it, girls.
More light, you knaves, and turn the tables up,
And quench the fire; the room is grown too hot.
Ah, sirrah, this unlooked-for sport comes well.
Nay, sit; nay, sit, good cousin Capulet;
For you and I are past our dancing days.
How long is't now since last yourself and I
Were in a mask?

Second Capulet.	By'r Lady, thirty years.
Capulet.	What, man? 'Tis not so much, 'tis not so much;
	'Tis since the nuptial of Lucentio,
	Come Pentecost as quickly as it will,
	Some five-and-twenty years, and then we masked.
Second Capulet.	'Tis more, 'tis more. His son is elder, sir;
	His son is thirty.
Capulet.	Will you tell me that?
	His son was but a ward two years ago.
Romeo.	[*To a Servingman*] What lady's that which
	doth enrich the hand
	Of yonder knight?
Servingman.	I know not, sir.
Romeo.	O, she doth teach the torches to burn bright!
	It seems she hangs upon the cheek of night
	As a rich jewel in an Ethiop's ear—
	Beauty too rich for use, for earth too dear!
	So shows a snowy dove trooping with crows
	As yonder lady o'er her fellows shows.
	The measure done, I'll watch her place of stand
	And, touching hers, make blessèd my rude hand.
	Did my heart love till now? Forswear it, sight!
	For I ne'er saw true beauty till this night.

Tybalt.	This, by his voice, should be a Montague.
	Fetch me my rapier, boy. What! Dares the slave
	Come hither, covered with an antic face,
	To fleer and scorn at our solemnity?
	Now, by the stock and honor of my kin,
	To strike him dead I hold it not a sin.
Capulet.	Why, how now, kinsman? Wherefore storm you so?
Tybalt.	Uncle, this is a Montague, our foe,
	A villain, that is hither come in spite
	To scorn at our solemnity this night.
Capulet.	Young Romeo is it ?
Tybalt.	'Tis he, that villain Romeo.
Capulet.	Content thee, gentle coz, let him alone.
	'A bears him like a portly gentleman,
	And, to say truth, Verona brags of him
	To be a virtuous and well-governed youth.
	I would not for the wealth of all this town
	Here in my house do him disparagement.
	Therefore be patient; take no note of him.
	It is my will, the which if thou respect,
	Show a fair presence and put off these frowns,
	An ill-beseeming semblance for a feast.

Tybalt.	It fits when such a villain is a guest.
	I'll not endure him.
Capulet.	He shall be endured.
	What, goodman boy! I say he shall. Go to!
	Am I the master here, or you? Go to!
	You'll not endure him, God shall mend my soul!
	You'll make a mutiny among my guests!
	You will set cock-a-hoop. You'll be the man!
Tybalt.	Why, uncle, 'tis a shame.
Capulet.	Go to, go to!
	You are a saucy boy. Is't so, indeed?
	This trick may chance to scathe you. I know what.
	You must contrary me! Marry, 'tis time—
	Well said, my hearts!—You are a princox—go!
	Be quiet, or—More light, more light!—For shame!
	I'll make you quiet. What!—Cheerly, my hearts!
Tybalt.	Patience perforce with willful choler meeting
	Makes my flesh tremble in their different greeting.
	I will withdraw; but this intrusion shall,
	Now seeming sweet, convert to bitt'rest gall.
	[*Exit*]

Romeo. If I profane with my unworthiest hand
This holy shrine, the gentle sin is this:
My lips, two blushing pilgrims, ready stand
To smooth that rough touch with a tender kiss.

Juliet. Good pilgrim, you do wrong your hand too much,
Which mannerly devotion shows in this;
For saints have hands that pilgrims' hands do touch,
And palm to palm is holy palmers' kiss.

Romeo. Have not saints lips, and holy palmers too?

Juliet. Ay, pilgrim, lips that they must use in prayer.

Romeo. O, then, dear saint, let lips do what hands do!
They pray; grant thou, lest faith turn to despair.

Juliet. Saints do not move, though grant for prayers' sake.

Romeo. Then move not while my prayer's effect I take.
Thus from my lips, by thine my sin is purged.
          [*Kisses her*]

Juliet. Then have my lips the sin that they have took.

Romeo.   Sin from my lips? O trespass sweetly urged!
          Give me my sin again.
             [*Kisses her*]
Juliet.   You kiss by th' book.
Nurse.   Madam, your mother craves a word with you.
Romeo.   What is her mother?
Nurse.   Marry, bachelor,
          Her mother is the lady of the house,
          And a good lady, and a wise and virtuous.
          I nursed her daughter that you talked withal.
          I tell you, he that can lay hold of her
          Shall have the chinks.
Romeo.   Is she a Capulet?
          O dear account! My life is my foe's debt.
Benvolio. Away, be gone; the sport is at the best.
Romeo.   Ay, so I fear; the more is my unrest.

Capulet. Nay, gentlemen, prepare not to be gone;
We have a trifling foolish banquet towards.
Is it e'en so? Why then, I thank you all.
I thank you, honest gentlemen. Good night.
More torches here! Come on then; let's to bed.
Ah, sirrah, by my fay, it waxes late;
I'll to my rest.

[*Exeunt all but Juliet and Nurse*]

Juliet. Come hither, nurse. What is yond gentleman?

Nurse. The son and heir of old Tiberio.

Juliet. What's he that now is going out of door?

Nurse. Marry, that, I think, be young Petruchio.

Juliet. What's he that follows here, that would not dance?

Nurse. I know not.

Juliet. Go ask his name.—If he is marrièd,
My grave is like to be my wedding bed.

Nurse. His name is Romeo, and a Montague,
The only son of your great enemy.

Juliet. My only love, sprung from my only hate!
Too early seen unknown, and known too late!
Prodigious birth of love it is to me
That I must love a loathèd enemy.

Nurse. What's this? What's this?

Juliet.   A rhyme I learnt even now
Of one I danced withal.
[*One calls within*], "Juliet."

Nurse.   Anon, anon!
Come, let's away; the strangers all are gone.
    [*Exeunt*]

ACT TWO

JULIƎT

PROLOGUE

[Enter Chorus]

Chorus.   Now old desire doth in his deathbed lie,

And young affection gapes to be his heir;

That fair for which love groaned for and would die,

With tender Juliet matched, is now not fair.

Now Romeo is beloved and loves again,

Alike bewitchèd by the charm of looks;

But to his foe supposed he must complain,

And she steal love's sweet bait from fearful hooks.

Being held a foe, he may not have access

To breathe such vows as lovers use to swear,

And she as much in love, her means much less

To meet her new belovèd anywhere;

But passion lends them power, time means, to meet,

Temp'ring extremities with extreme sweet.

[Exit]

[Enter Romeo alone]

Romeo.   Can I go forward when my heart is here?

Turn back, dull earth, and find thy center out.

[Enter Benvolio with Mercutio. Romeo retires]

Benvolio.   Romeo! My cousin Romeo! Romeo!

Mercutio.   He is wise

And, on my life, hath stol'n him home to bed.

Benvolio.   He ran this way and leapt this orchard wall.

Call, good Mercutio.

Mercutio.   Nay, I'll conjure too.

Romeo! Humors! Madman! Passion! Lover!

Appear thou in the likeness of a sigh;

Speak but one rhyme, and I am satisfied!

Cry but "Ay me!" pronounce but "love" and "dove";

Speak to my gossip Venus one fair word,

One nickname for her purblind son and heir,
Young Abraham Cupid, he that shot so true
When King Cophetua loved the beggar maid!
He heareth not, he stirreth not, he moveth not;
The ape is dead, and I must conjure him.
I conjure thee by Rosaline's bright eyes,
By her high forehead and her scarlet lip,
By her fine foot, straight leg, and quivering thigh,
And the demesnes that there adjacent lie,
That in thy likeness thou appear to us!

Benvolio. And if he hear thee, thou wilt anger him.

Mercutio. This cannot anger him. 'Twould anger him
To raise a spirit in his mistress' circle
Of some strange nature, letting it there stand
Till she had laid it and conjured it down.
That were some spite; my invocation
Is fair and honest: in his mistress' name,
I conjure only but to raise up him.

Benvolio. Come, he hath hid himself among these trees
To be consorted with the humorous night.
Blind is his love and best befits the dark.

Mercutio. If love be blind, love cannot hit the mark.
Now will he sit under a medlar tree
And wish his mistress were that kind of fruit
As maids call medlars when they laugh alone.
O, Romeo, that she were, O that she were
An open *et cetera,* thou a pop'rin pear!
Romeo, good night. I'll to my truckle bed;
This field bed is too cold for me to sleep.
Come, shall we go?

Benvolio. Go then, for 'tis in vain
To seek him here that means not to be found.

[*Exit with others*]

SCENE II
CAPULET'S ORCHARD

[Romeo, coming forward]

Romeo.   He jests at scars that never felt a wound.

    [Enter Juliet at a window]

But soft! What light through yonder window breaks?

It is the East, and Juliet is the sun!

Arise, fair sun, and kill the envious moon,

Who is already sick and pale with grief

That thou her maid art far more fair than she.

Be not her maid, since she is envious.

Her vestal livery is but sick and green,

And none but fools do wear it. Cast it off.

It is my lady! O, it is my love!

O, that she knew she were!

She speaks, yet she says nothing. What of that?

Her eye discourses; I will answer it.

I am too bold; 'tis not to me she speaks.
Two of the fairest stars in all the heaven,
Having some business, do entreat her eyes
To twinkle in their spheres till they return.
What if her eyes were there, they in her head?
The brightness of her cheek would shame those stars
As daylight doth a lamp; her eyes in heaven
Would through the airy region stream so bright
That birds would sing and think it were not night.
See how she leans her cheek upon her hand!
O, that I were a glove upon that hand,
That I might touch that cheek!

Juliet.   Ay me!

Romeo.   She speaks.

O, speak again, bright angel, for thou art
As glorious to this night, being o'er my head,
As is a wingèd messenger of heaven
Unto the white-upturnèd wond'ring eyes
Of mortals that fall back to gaze on him
When he bestrides the lazy puffing clouds
And sails upon the bosom of the air.

Juliet. O Romeo, Romeo! Wherefore art thou Romeo?
Deny thy father and refuse thy name;
Or, if thou wilt not, be but sworn my love,
And I'll no longer be a Capulet.

Romeo. [*Aside*] Shall I hear more, or shall I speak at this?

Juliet. 'Tis but thy name that is my enemy.
Thou art thyself, though not a Montague.
What's Montague? It is nor hand, nor foot,
Nor arm, nor face. O, be some other name
Belonging to a man.
What's in a name? That which we call a rose
By any other word would smell as sweet.
So Romeo would, were he not Romeo called,
Retain that dear perfection which he owes
Without that title. Romeo, doff thy name;
And for thy name, which is no part of thee,
Take all myself.

Romeo.	I take thee at thy word.
	Call me but love, and I'll be new baptized;
	Henceforth I never will be Romeo.
Juliet.	What man art thou, that, thus bescreened in night,
	So stumblest on my counsel?
Romeo.	By a name
	I know not how to tell thee who I am.
	My name, dear saint, is hateful to myself
	Because it is an enemy to thee.
	Had I it written, I would tear the word.
Juliet.	My ears have yet not drunk a hundred words
	Of thy tongue's uttering, yet I know the sound.
	Art thou not Romeo, and a Montague?
Romeo.	Neither, fair maid, if either thee dislike.
Juliet.	How camest thou hither, tell me, and wherefore?
	The orchard walls are high and hard to climb,
	And the place death, considering who thou art,
	If any of my kinsmen find thee here.

Romeo.	With love's light wings did I o'erperch these walls;
	For stony limits cannot hold love out,
	And what love can do, that dares love attempt.
	Therefore thy kinsmen are no stop to me.
Juliet.	If they do see thee, they will murder thee.
Romeo.	Alack, there lies more peril in thine eye
	Than twenty of their swords! Look thou but sweet,
	And I am proof against their enmity.
Juliet.	I would not for the world they saw thee here.
Romeo.	I have night's cloak to hide me from their eyes;
	And but thou love me, let them find me here.
	My life were better ended by their hate
	Than death proroguèd, wanting of thy love.
Juliet.	By whose direction found'st thou out this place?
Romeo.	By love, that first did prompt me to inquire.
	He lent me counsel, and I lent him eyes.
	I am no pilot; yet, wert thou as far
	As that vast shore washed with the farthest sea,
	I should adventure for such merchandise.

Juliet. Thou knowest the mask of night is on my face;
Else would a maiden blush bepaint my cheek
For that which thou hast heard me speak tonight.
Fain would I dwell on form—fain, fain deny
What I have spoke; but farewell compliment!
Dost thou love me? I know thou wilt say "Ay";
And I will take thy word. Yet, if thou swear'st,
Thou mayst prove false. At lovers' perjuries,
They say Jove laughs. O gentle Romeo,
If thou dost love, pronounce it faithfully.
Or if thou thinkest I am too quickly won,
I'll frown and be perverse and say thee nay,
So thou wilt woo; but else, not for the world.
In truth, fair Montague, I am too fond,
And therefore thou mayst think my havior light;
But trust me, gentleman, I'll prove more true
Than those that have more cunning to be strange.
I should have been more strange, I must confess,
But that thou overheard'st, ere I was ware,
My truelove passion. Therefore pardon me,
And not impute this yielding to light love,
Which the dark night hath so discoverèd.

Romeo. Lady, by yonder blessèd moon I vow,
That tips with silver all these fruit-tree tops—
Juliet. O, swear not by the moon, th' inconstant moon,
That monthly changes in her circle orb,
Lest that thy love prove likewise variable.
Romeo. What shall I swear by?
Juliet.   Do not swear at all;
Or if thou wilt, swear by thy gracious self,
Which is the god of my idolatry,
And I'll believe thee.
Romeo.   If my heart's dear love—
Juliet. Well, do not swear. Although I joy in thee,
I have no joy of this contract tonight.
It is too rash, too unadvised, too sudden;
Too like the lightning, which doth cease to be
Ere one can say it lightens. Sweet, good night!
This bud of love, by summer's ripening breath,
May prove a beauteous flow'r when next we meet.
Good night, good night! As sweet repose and rest
Come to thy heart as that within my breast!

Romeo.	O, wilt thou leave me so unsatisfied?
Juliet.	What satisfaction canst thou have tonight?
Romeo.	Th' exchange of thy love's faithful vow for mine.
Juliet.	I gave thee mine before thou didst request it;
	And yet I would it were to give again.
Romeo.	Wouldst thou withdraw it? For what purpose, love?
Juliet.	But to be frank and give it thee again.
	And yet I wish but for the thing I have.
	My bounty is as boundless as the sea,
	My love as deep; the more I give to thee,
	The more I have, for both are infinite.
	I hear some noise within. Dear love, adieu!

     [*Nurse calls within*]

    Anon, good nurse! Sweet Montague, be true.

    Stay but a little, I will come again.

     [*Exit*]

Romeo.	O blessèd, blessèd night! I am afeard,
	Being in night, all this is but a dream,
	Too flattering-sweet to be substantial.
	[*Enter Juliet again*]
Juliet.	Three words, dear Romeo, and good night indeed.
	If that thy bent of love be honorable,
	Thy purpose marriage, send me word tomorrow,
	By one that I'll procure to come to thee,
	Where and what time thou wilt perform the rite;
	And all my fortunes at thy foot I'll lay
	And follow thee my lord throughout the world.
Nurse.	[*Within*] Madam!
Juliet.	I come anon.—But if thou meanest not well,
	I do beseech thee—
Nurse.	[*Within*] Madam!
Juliet.	By and by I come.—
	To cease thy strife and leave me to my grief.
	Tomorrow will I send.
Romeo.	So thrive my soul—

Juliet. A thousand times good night!

[*Exit*]

Romeo. A thousand times the worse, to want thy light!

Love goes toward love as schoolboys from their books;

But love from love, toward school with heavy looks.

[*Enter Juliet again*]

Juliet. Hist! Romeo, hist! O for a falc'ner's voice

To lure this tassel gentle back again!

Bondage is hoarse and may not speak aloud,

Else would I tear the cave where Echo lies

And make her airy tongue more hoarse than mine

With repetition of "My Romeo!"

Romeo. It is my soul that calls upon my name.

How silver-sweet sound lovers' tongues by night,

Like softest music to attending ears!

Juliet. Romeo!

Romeo. My sweet?

Juliet. What o'clock tomorrow

Shall I send to thee?

Romeo. By the hour of nine.

Juliet. I will not fail. 'Tis twenty year till then.

I have forgot why I did call thee back.

Romeo. Let me stand here till thou remember it.

Juliet. I shall forget, to have thee still stand there,
Rememb'ring how I love thy company.

Romeo. And I'll still stay, to have thee still forget,
Forgetting any other home but this.

Juliet. 'Tis almost morning. I would have thee gone—
And yet no farther than a wanton's bird,
That lets it hop a little from his hand,
Like a poor prisoner in his twisted gyves,
And with a silken thread plucks it back again,
So loving-jealous of his liberty.

Romeo. I would I were thy bird.

Juliet.   Sweet, so would I.
Yet I should kill thee with much cherishing.
Good night, good night! Parting is such sweet sorrow
That I shall say good night till it be morrow.
[*Exit*]

Romeo. Sleep dwell upon thine eyes, peace in thy breast!
Would I were sleep and peace, so sweet to rest!
Hence will I to my ghostly friar's close cell,
His help to crave and my dear hap to tell.
[*Exit*]

[Enter Friar Lawrence alone, with a basket]

Friar.   The gray-eyed morn smiles on the frowning night,
Check'ring the eastern clouds with streaks of light;
And fleckèd darkness like a drunkard reels
From forth day's path and Titan's burning wheels.
Now, ere the sun advance his burning eye
The day to cheer and night's dank dew to dry,
I must upfill this osier cage of ours
With baleful weeds and precious-juicèd flowers.
The earth that's nature's mother is her tomb.
What is her burying grave, that is her womb;
And from her womb children of divers kind
We sucking on her natural bosom find,
Many for many virtues excellent,

None but for some, and yet all different.
O, mickle is the powerful grace that lies
In plants, herbs, stones, and their true qualities;
For naught so vile that on the earth doth live
But to the earth some special good doth give;
Nor aught so good but, strained from that fair use,
Revolts from true birth, stumbling on abuse.
Virtue itself turns vice, being misapplied,
And vice sometime by action dignified.
    [*Enter Romeo*]
Within the infant rind of this weak flower
Poison hath residence and medicine power;
For this, being smelt, with that part cheers each part;
Being tasted, stays all senses with the heart.
Two such opposèd kings encamp them still
In man as well as herbs—grace and rude will;
And where the worser is predominant,
Full soon the canker death eats up that plant.

Romeo.   Good morrow, father.

Friar.   *Benedicite!*

What early tongue so sweet saluteth me?
Young son, it argues a distemperèd head
So soon to bid good morrow to thy bed.
Care keeps his watch in every old man's eye,
And where care lodges, sleep will never lie;
But where unbruisèd youth with unstuffed brain
Doth couch his limbs, there golden sleep doth reign.
Therefore thy earliness doth me assure
Thou art uproused with some distemp'rature;
Or if not so, then here I hit it right—
Our Romeo hath not been in bed tonight.

Romeo.   That last is true. The sweeter rest was mine.

Friar.   God pardon sin! Wast thou with Rosaline?

Romeo.   With Rosaline, my ghostly father? No.
I have forgot that name and that name's woe.

Friar.   That's my good son! But where hast thou been then?

ESCALUS

Romeo.	I'll tell thee ere thou ask it me again.
	I have been feasting with mine enemy,
	Where on a sudden one hath wounded me
	That's by me wounded. Both our remedies
	Within thy help and holy physic lies.
	I bear no hatred, blessèd man, for, lo,
	My intercession likewise steads my foe.
Friar.	Be plain, good son, and homely in thy drift.
	Riddling confession finds but riddling shrift.
Romeo.	Then plainly know my heart's dear love is set
	On the fair daughter of rich Capulet;
	As mine on hers, so hers is set on mine,
	And all combined, save what thou must combine
	By holy marriage. When and where and how
	We met, we wooed, and made exchange of vow,
	I'll tell thee as we pass; but this I pray,
	That thou consent to marry us today.

Friar.	Holy Saint Francis! What a change is here!
	Is Rosaline, that thou didst love so dear,
	So soon forsaken? Young men's love then lies
	Not truly in their hearts, but in their eyes.
	Jesu Maria! What a deal of brine
	Hath washed thy sallow cheeks for Rosaline!
	How much salt water thrown away in waste
	To season love, that of it doth not taste!
	The sun not yet thy sighs from heaven clears,
	Thy old groans ring yet in mine ancient ears.
	Lo, here upon thy cheek the stain doth sit
	Of an old tear that is not washed off yet.
	If e'er thou wast thyself, and these woes thine,
	Thou and these woes were all for Rosaline.
	And art thou changed? Pronounce this sentence then:
	Women may fall when there's no strength in men.
Romeo.	Thou chidst me oft for loving Rosaline.
Friar.	For doting, not for loving, pupil mine.

Romeo. And badst me bury love.

Friar.   Not in a grave
To lay one in, another out to have.

Romeo. I pray thee chide me not. Her I love now
Doth grace for grace and love for love allow.
The other did not so.

Friar.   O, she knew well
Thy love did read by rote, that could not spell.
But come, young waverer, come go with me.
In one respect I'll thy assistant be;
For this alliance may so happy prove
To turn your households' rancor to pure love.

Romeo. O, let us hence! I stand on sudden haste.

Friar. Wisely and slow. They stumble that run fast.
                    [*Exeunt*]

SCENE IV
A STREET

[Enter Benvolio and Mercutio]

Mercutio. Where the devil should this Romeo be?
Came he not home tonight?

Benvolio. Not to his father's. I spoke with his man.

Mercutio. Why, that same pale hardhearted wench, that Rosaline,
Torments him so that he will sure run mad.

Benvolio. Tybalt, the kinsman to old Capulet,
Hath sent a letter to his father's house.

Mercutio. A challenge, on my life.

Benvolio. Romeo will answer it.

Mercutio. Any man that can write may answer a letter.

Benvolio. Nay, he will answer the letter's master, how he
dares, being dared.

Mercutio. Alas, poor Romeo, he is already dead: stabbed
with a white wench's black eye; run through
the ear with a love song; the very pin of his
heart cleft with the blind bow-boy's butt-shaft;
and is he a man to encounter Tybalt?

Benvolio. Why, what is Tybalt?

Mercutio. More than Prince of Cats. O, he's the courageous captain of compliments. He fights as you sing pricksong—keeps time, distance, and proportion; he rests his minim rests, one, two, and the third in your bosom! The very butcher of a silk button, a duelist, a duelist! A gentleman of the very first house, of the first and second cause. Ah, the immortal *passado!* The *punto reverso!* The hay!

Benvolio. The what?

Mercutio. The pox of such antic, lisping, affecting fantasticoes—these new tuners of accent! "By Jesu, a very good blade! A very tall man! A very good whore!" Why, is not this a lamentable thing, grandsir, that we should be thus afflicted with these strange flies, these fashionmongers, these pardon-me's, who stand so much on the new form that they cannot sit at ease on the old bench? O, their bones, their bones!

[*Enter Romeo*]

Benvolio.	Here comes Romeo! Here comes Romeo!
Mercutio.	Without his roe, like a dried herring. O flesh, flesh, how art thou fishified! Now is he for the numbers that Petrarch flowed in. Laura, to his lady, was a kitchen wench (marry, she had a better love to berhyme her), Dido a dowdy, Cleopatra a gypsy, Helen and Hero hildings and harlots, Thisbe a gray eye or so, but not to the purpose. Signior Romeo, *bon jour!* There's a French salutation to your French slop. You gave us the counterfeit fairly last night.
Romeo.	Good morrow to you both. What counterfeit did I give you?
Mercutio.	The slip, sir, the slip. Can you not conceive?
Romeo.	Pardon, good Mercutio. My business was great, and in such a case as mine a man may strain courtesy.
Mercutio.	That's as much as to say, such a case as yours constrains a man to bow in the hams.

Romeo.	Meaning, to curtsy.
Mercutio.	Thou hast most kindly hit it.
Romeo.	A most courteous exposition.
Mercutio.	Nay, I am the very pink of courtesy.
Romeo.	Pink for flower.
Mercutio.	Right.
Romeo.	Why, then is my pump well-flowered.
Mercutio.	Sure wit, follow me this jest now till thou hast worn out thy pump, that, when the single sole of it is worn, the jest may remain, after the wearing, solely singular.
Romeo.	O single-soled jest, solely singular for the singleness!
Mercutio.	Come between us, good Benvolio! My wits faints.
Romeo.	Swits and spurs, swits and spurs; or I'll cry a match.
Mercutio.	Nay, if our wits run the wild-goose chase, I am done; for thou hast more of the wild goose in one of thy wits than, I am sure, I have in my whole five. Was I with you there for the goose?

Romeo. Thou wast never with me for anything when thou wast not there for the goose.

Mercutio. I will bite thee by the ear for that jest.

Romeo. Nay, good goose, bite not!

Mercutio. Thy wit is a very bitter sweeting; it is a most sharp sauce.

Romeo. And is it not, then, well served in to a sweet goose?

Mercutio. O, here's a wit of cheveril, that stretches from an inch narrow to an ell broad!

Romeo. I stretch it out for that word "broad," which added to the goose, proves thee far and wide a broad goose.

Mercutio. Why, is not this better now than groaning for love? Now art thou sociable, now art thou Romeo; now art thou what thou art, by art as well as by nature. For this driveling love is like a great natural that runs lolling up and down to hide his bauble in a hole.

Benvolio. Stop there, stop there!

Mercutio. Thou desirest me to stop in my tale against the hair.

Benvolio.	Thou wouldst else have made thy tale large.
Mercutio.	O, thou art deceived! I would have made it short; for I was come to the whole depth of my tale, and meant indeed to occupy the argument no longer.
Romeo.	Here's goodly gear!

[*Enter Nurse and her Man, Peter*]

	A sail, a sail!
Mercutio.	Two, two! A shirt and a smock.
Nurse.	Peter!
Peter.	Anon.
Nurse.	My fan, Peter.
Mercutio.	Good Peter, to hide her face; for her fan's the fairer face.
Nurse.	God ye good morrow, gentlemen.
Mercutio.	God ye good-den, fair gentlewoman.
Nurse.	Is it good-den?
Mercutio.	'Tis no less, I tell ye; for the bawdy hand of the dial is now upon the prick of noon.
Nurse.	Out upon you! What a man are you!

Romeo.	One, gentlewoman, that God hath made, himself to mar.
Nurse.	By my troth, it is well said. "For himself to mar," quoth 'a? Gentlemen, can any of you tell me where I may find the young Romeo?
Romeo.	I can tell you; but young Romeo will be older when you have found him than he was when you sought him. I am the youngest of that name, for fault of a worse.
Nurse.	You say well.
Mercutio.	Yea, is the worst well? Very well took, i' faith! Wisely, wisely.
Nurse.	If you be he, sir, I desire some confidence with you.
Benvolio.	She will endite him to some supper.
Mercutio.	A bawd, a bawd, a bawd! So ho!
Romeo.	What hast thou found?

NURSE

Mercutio. No hare, sir; unless a hare, sir, in a lenten pie, that is something stale and hoar ere it be spent.

[*He walks by them*]

[*Sings*] An old hare hoar,
And an old hare hoar,
Is very good meat in Lent;
But a hare that is hoar
Is too much for a score
When it hoars ere it be spent.

Romeo, will you come to your father's? We'll to dinner thither.

Romeo. I will follow you.

Mercutio. Farewell, ancient lady. Farwell,

[*Sings*] "Lady, lady, lady."

[*Exeunt Mercutio, Benvolio*]

Nurse. I pray you, sir, what saucy merchant was this that was so full of his ropery?

Romeo. A gentleman, nurse, that loves to hear himself talk and will speak more in a minute than he will stand to in a month.

Nurse. And 'a speak anything against me, I'll take him down, and 'a were lustier than he is, and twenty such Jacks; and if I cannot, I'll find those that shall. Scurvy knave! I am none of his flirt-gills; I am none of his skainsmates. And thou must stand by too, and suffer every knave to use me at his pleasure!

Peter. I saw no man use you at his pleasure. If I had, my weapon should quickly have been out, I warrant you. I dare draw as soon as another man, if I see occasion in a good quarrel, and the law on my side.

Nurse. Now, afore God, I am so vexed that every part about me quivers. Scurvy knave! Pray you, sir, a word; and, as I told you, my young lady bid me inquire you out. What she bid me say, I will keep to myself; but first let me tell ye, if ye should lead her in a fool's paradise, as they say, it were a very gross kind of behavior, as they say; for the gentlewoman is young; and therefore, if you should deal double with her, truly it were an ill thing to be off'red to any gentlewoman, and very weak dealing.

Romeo. Nurse, commend me to thy lady and mistress.
I protest unto thee—

Nurse. Good heart, and i' faith I will tell her as much.
Lord, Lord, she will be a joyful woman.

Romeo. What wilt thou tell her, nurse? Thou dost not
mark me.

Nurse. I will tell her, sir, that you do protest, which, as
I take it, is a gentlemanlike offer.

Romeo. Bid her devise
Some means to come to shrift this afternoon;
And there she shall at Friar Lawrence' cell
Be shrived and married. Here is for thy pains.

Nurse. No, truly, sir; not a penny.

Romeo. Go to! I say you shall.

Nurse. This afternoon, sir? Well, she shall be there.

Romeo. And stay, good nurse, behind the abbey wall.
Within this hour my man shall be with thee
And bring thee cords made like a tackled stair,
Which to the high topgallant of my joy
Must be my convoy in the secret night.
Farewell. Be trusty, and I'll quit thy pains.
Farewell. Commend me to thy mistress.

Nurse. Now God in heaven bless thee! Hark you, sir.

Romeo. What say'st thou, my dear nurse?

Nurse. Is your man secret? Did you ne'er hear say,
Two may keep counsel, putting one away?

Romeo. Warrant thee my man's as true as steel.

Nurse. Well, sir, my mistress is the sweetest lady. Lord,
Lord! When 'twas a little prating thing—O,
there is a nobleman in town, one Paris, that
would fain lay knife aboard; but she, good soul,
had as lieve see a toad, a very toad, as see him.
I anger her sometimes, and tell her that Paris
is the properer man; but I'll warrant you, when
I say so, she looks as pale as any clout in the
versal world. Doth not rosemary and Romeo
begin both with a letter?

Romeo. Ay, nurse; what of that? Both with an *R*.

Nurse. Ah, mocker! That's the dog's name. *R* is for the—No; I know it begins with some other letter; and she hath the prettiest sententious of it, of you and rosemary, that it would do you good to hear it.

Romeo. Commend me to thy lady.

Nurse. Ay, a thousand times.

       [*Exit Romeo*]

                      Peter!

Peter. Anon.

Nurse. Before, and apace.

       [*Exit after Peter*]

SCENE V

CAPULET'S ORCHARD

[*Enter Juliet*]

Juliet.   The clock struck nine when I did send the nurse;
In half an hour she promised to return.
Perchance she cannot meet him. That's not so.
O, she is lame! Love's heralds should be thoughts,
Which ten times faster glides than the sun's beams
Driving back shadows over low'ring hills.
Therefore do nimble-pinioned doves draw Love,
And therefore hath the wind-swift Cupid wings.
Now is the sun upon the highmost hill
Of this day's journey, and from nine till twelve
Is three long hours; yet she is not come.
Had she affections and warm youthful blood,
She would be as swift in motion as a ball;
My words would bandy her to my sweet love,
And his to me.
But old folks, many feign as they were dead—
Unwieldy, slow, heavy and pale as lead.

[*Enter Nurse and Peter*]

O God, she comes! O honey nurse, what news?
Hast thou met with him? Send thy man away.

Nurse.	Peter, stay at the gate.
	[*Exit Peter*]
Juliet.	Now, good sweet nurse—O Lord, why lookest thou sad?
	Though news be sad, yet tell them merrily;
	If good, thou shamest the music of sweet news
	By playing it to me with so sour a face.
Nurse.	I am aweary, give me leave awhile.
	Fie, how my bones ache! What a jaunce have I!
Juliet.	I would thou hadst my bones, and I thy news.
	Nay, come, I pray thee speak. Good, good nurse, speak.
Nurse.	Jesu, what haste! Can you not stay awhile?
	Do you not see that I am out of breath?
Juliet.	How art thou out of breath when thou hast breath
	To say to me that thou art out of breath?
	The excuse that thou dost make in this delay
	Is longer than the tale thou dost excuse.
	Is thy news good or bad? Answer to that.
	Say either, and I'll stay the circumstance.
	Let me be satisfied, is't good or bad?

Nurse. Well, you have made a simple choice; you know
not how to choose a man. Romeo? No, not he.
Though his face be better than any man's, yet
his leg excels all men's; and for a hand and a
foot, and a body, though they be not to be
talked on, yet they are past compare. He is not
the flower of courtesy, but, I'll warrant him, as
gentle as a lamb. Go thy ways, wench; serve
God. What, have you dined at home?

Juliet. No, no. But all this did I know before.
What says he of our marriage? What of that?

Nurse. Lord, how my head aches! What a head have I!
It beats as it would fall in twenty pieces.
My back a t' other side—ah, my back, my back!
Beshrew your heart for sending me about
To catch my death with jauncing up and down!

Juliet. I' faith, I am sorry that thou art not well.
Sweet, sweet, sweet nurse, tell me, what says my love?

Nurse. Your love says, like an honest gentleman, and,
a courteous, and a kind, and a handsome, and,
I warrant, a virtuous—Where is your mother?

Juliet.   Where is my mother? Why, she is within.

Where should she be? How oddly thou repliest!

"Your love says, like an honest gentleman,

'Where is your mother?' "

Nurse.   O God's Lady dear!

Are you so hot? Marry come up, I trow.

Is this the poultice for my aching bones?

Henceforward do your messages yourself.

Juliet.   Here's such a coil! Come, what says Romeo?

Nurse.   Have you got leave to go to shrift today?

Juliet.   I have.

Nurse.   Then hie you hence to Friar Lawrence' cell;

There stays a husband to make you a wife.

Now comes the wanton blood up in your cheeks:

They'll be in scarlet straight at any news.

Hie you to church; I must another way,

To fetch a ladder, by the which your love

Must climb a bird's nest soon when it is dark.

I am the drudge, and toil in your delight;

But you shall bear the burden soon at night.

Go; I'll to dinner; hie you to the cell.

Juliet.   Hie to high fortune! Honest nurse, farewell.

      [*Exeunt*]

SCENE VI
FRIAR LAWRENCE'S CELL

[Enter Friar Lawrence and Romeo]

Friar. So smile the heavens upon this holy act
That afterhours with sorrow chide us not!

Romeo. Amen, amen! But come what sorrow can,
It cannot countervail the exchange of joy
That one short minute gives me in her sight.
Do thou but close our hands with holy words,
Then love-devouring death do what he dare—
It is enough I may but call her mine.

Friar. These violent delights have violent ends
And in their triumph die, like fire and powder,
Which, as they kiss, consume. The sweetest honey
Is loathsome in his own deliciousness
And in the taste confounds the appetite.
Therefore love moderately: long love doth so;
Too swift arrives as tardy as too slow.

[Enter Juliet]

Here comes the lady. O, so light a foot
Will ne'er wear out the everlasting flint.
A lover may bestride the gossamers
That idles in the wanton summer air,
And yet not fall; so light is vanity.

Juliet. Good even to my ghostly confessor.

Friar. Romeo shall thank thee, daughter, for us both.

Juliet. As much to him, else is his thanks too much.

Romeo. Ah, Juliet, if the measure of thy joy
Be heaped like mine, and that thy skill be more
To blazon it, then sweeten with thy breath
This neighbor air, and let rich music's tongue
Unfold the imagined happiness that both
Receive in either by this dear encounter.

Juliet. Conceit, more rich in matter than in words,
Brags of his substance, not of ornament.
They are but beggars that can count their worth;
But my true love is grown to such excess
I cannot sum up sum of half my wealth.

Friar. Come, come with me, and we will make short work;
For, by your leaves, you shall not stay alone
Till Holy Church incorporate two in one.

[Exeunt]

ACT THREE

PARIS

A PUBLIC PLACE

[*Enter Mercutio, Benvolio, and Men*]

Benvolio. I pray thee, good Mercutio, let's retire.
The day is hot, the Capels are abroad,
And, if we meet, we shall not 'scape a brawl,
For now, these hot days, is the mad blood stirring.

Mercutio. Thou art like one of these fellows that, when
he enters the confines of a tavern, claps me his
sword upon the table and says, "God send me
no need of thee!" and by the operation of the
second cup draws him on the drawer, when indeed there is no need.

Benvolio. Am I like such a fellow?

Mercutio. Come, come, thou art as hot a Jack in thy mood
as any in Italy; and as soon moved to be moody,
and as soon moody to be moved.

Benvolio. And what to?

Mercutio. Nay, and there were two such, we should have none shortly, for one would kill the other. Thou! Why, thou wilt quarrel with a man that hath a hair more or a hair less in his beard than thou hast. Thou wilt quarrel with a man for cracking nuts, having no other reason but because thou hast hazel eyes. What eye but such an eye would spy out such a quarrel? Thy head is as full of quarrels as an egg is full of meat; and yet thy head hath been beaten as addle as an egg for quarreling. Thou hast quarreled with a man for coughing in the street, because he hath wakened thy dog that hath lain asleep in the sun. Didst thou not fall out with a tailor for wearing his new doublet before Easter? With another for tying his new shoes with old riband? And yet thou wilt tutor me from quarreling!

Benvolio. And I were so apt to quarrel as thou art, any man should buy the fee simple of my life for an hour and a quarter.

Mercutio. The fee simple? O simple!

> [*Enter Tybalt, Petruchio, and others*]

Benvolio. By my head, here comes the Capulets.

Mercutio.	By my heel, I care not.
Tybalt.	Follow me close, for I will speak to them.
	Gentlemen, good-den. A word with one of you.
Mercutio.	And but one word with one of us? Couple it with something; make it a word and a blow.
Tybalt.	You shall find me apt enough to that, sir, and you will give me occasion.
Mercutio.	Could you not take some occasion without giving?
Tybalt.	Mercutio, thou consortest with Romeo.
Mercutio.	Consort? What, dost thou make us minstrels? And thou make minstrels of us, look to hear nothing but discords. Here's my fiddlestick; here's that shall make you dance. Zounds, consort!
Benvolio.	We talk here in the public haunt of men. Either withdraw unto some private place, Or reason coldly of your grievances, Or else depart. Here all eyes gaze on us.
Mercutio.	Men's eyes were made to look, and let them gaze. I will not budge for no man's pleasure, I.
	[*Enter Romeo*]
Tybalt.	Well, peace be with you, sir. Here comes my man.

Mercutio.	But I'll be hanged, sir, if he wear your livery.
	Marry, go before to field, he'll be your follower!
	Your worship in that sense may call him man.
Tybalt.	Romeo, the love I bear thee can afford
	No better term than this: thou art a villain.
Romeo.	Tybalt, the reason that I have to love thee
	Doth much excuse the appertaining rage
	To such a greeting. Villain am I none.
	Therefore farewell. I see thou knowest me not.
Tybalt.	Boy, this shall not excuse the injuries
	That thou hast done me; therefore turn and draw.
Romeo.	I do protest I never injured thee,
	But love thee better than thou canst devise
	Till thou shalt know the reason of my love;
	And so, good Capulet, which name I tender
	As dearly as mine own, be satisfied.
Mercutio.	O calm, dishonorable, vile submission!
	Alla stoccata carries it away.
	[*Draws*]
	Tybalt, you ratcatcher, will you walk?
Tybalt.	What wouldst thou have with me?

Mercutio. Good King of Cats, nothing but one of your nine lives. That I mean to make bold withal, and, as you shall use me hereafter, dry-beat the rest of the eight. Will you pluck your sword out of his pilcher by the ears? Make haste, lest mine be about your ears ere it be out.

Tybalt. I am for you.

    [Draws]

Romeo. Gentle Mercutio, put thy rapier up.

Mercutio. Come, sir, your *passado!*

    [They fight]

Romeo. Draw, Benvolio; beat down their weapons.
Gentlemen, for shame! Forbear this outrage!
Tybalt, Mercutio, the Prince expressly hath
Forbid this bandying in Verona streets.
Hold, Tybalt! Good Mercutio!

    [Tybalt, under Romeo's arm,
    thrusts Mercutio in, and flies]

Mercutio.   I am hurt.
A plague a both houses! I am sped.
Is he gone and hath nothing?

Benvolio.	What, art thou hurt?
Mercutio.	Ay, ay, a scratch, a scratch. Marry, 'tis enough. Where is my page? Go, villain, fetch a surgeon.

[*Exit Page*]

Romeo.	Courage, man. The hurt cannot be much.
Mercutio.	No, 'tis not so deep as a well, nor so wide as a church door; but 'tis enough, 'twill serve. Ask for me tomorrow, and you shall find me a grave man. I am peppered, I warrant, for this world. A plague a both your houses! Zounds, a dog, a rat, a mouse, a cat, to scratch a man to death! A braggart, a rogue, a villain, that fights by the book of arithmetic! Why the devil came you between us? I was hurt under your arm.
Romeo.	I thought all for the best.
Mercutio.	Help me into some house, Benvolio, Or I shall faint. A plague a both your houses! They have made worms' meat of me. I have it, And soundly too. Your houses!

[*Exeunt Mercutio and Benvolio*]

Romeo.	This gentleman, the Prince's near ally,

Romeo. This gentleman, the Prince's near ally,
My very friend, hath got this mortal hurt
In my behalf—my reputation stained
With Tybalt's slander—Tybalt, that an hour
Hath been my cousin. O sweet Juliet,
Thy beauty hath made me effeminate
And in my temper soft'ned valor's steel!
          [*Enter Benvolio*]

Benvolio. O Romeo, Romeo, brave Mercutio is dead!
That gallant spirit hath aspired the clouds,
Which too untimely here did scorn the earth.

Romeo. This day's black fate on moe days doth depend;
This but begins the woe others must end.
          [*Enter Tybalt*]

Benvolio. Here comes the furious Tybalt back again.

Romeo. Alive in triumph, and Mercutio slain?
Away to heaven respective lenity,
And fire-eyed fury be my conduct now!
Now, Tybalt, take the "villain" back again
That late thou gavest me; for Mercutio's soul
Is but a little way above our heads,
Staying for thine to keep him company.
Either thou or I, or both, must go with him.

Tybalt.	Thou, wretched boy, that didst consort him here,
	Shalt with him hence.
Romeo.	This shall determine that.
	[They fight. Tybalt falls]
Benvolio.	Romeo, away, be gone!
	The citizens are up, and Tybalt slain.
	Stand not amazed. The Prince will doom thee death
	If thou art taken. Hence, be gone, away!
Romeo.	O, I am fortune's fool!
Benvolio.	Why dost thou stay?
	[Exit Romeo]
	[Enter Citizens]
Citizen.	Which way ran he that killed Mercutio?
	Tybalt, that murderer, which way ran he?
Benvolio.	There lies that Tybalt.
Citizen.	Up, sir, go with me.
	I charge thee in the Prince's name obey.
	[Enter Prince, old Montague,
	Capulet, their Wives, and all]
Prince.	Where are the vile beginners of this fray?
Benvolio.	O noble Prince, I can discover all
	The unlucky manage of this fatal brawl.
	There lies the man, slain by young Romeo,
	That slew thy kinsman, brave Mercutio.

Lady Capulet.	Tybalt, my cousin! O my brother's child!
	O Prince! O cousin! Husband! O, the blood is spilled
	Of my dear kinsman! Prince, as thou art true,
	For blood of ours shed blood of Montague.
	O cousin, cousin!
Prince.	Benvolio, who began this bloody fray?
Benvolio.	Tybalt, here slain, whom Romeo's hand did slay.
	Romeo, that spoke him fair, bid him bethink
	How nice the quarrel was, and urged withal
	Your high displeasure. All this—utterèd
	With gentle breath, calm look, knees humbly bowed—
	Could not take truce with the unruly spleen
	Of Tybalt deaf to peace, but that he tilts
	With piercing steel at bold Mercutio's breast;
	Who, all as hot, turns deadly point to point,
	And, with a martial scorn, with one hand beats
	Cold death aside and with the other sends
	It back to Tybalt, whose dexterity

Retorts it. Romeo he cries aloud,
"Hold, friends! Friends, part!" and swifter than his tongue,
His agile arm beats down their fatal points,
And 'twixt them rushes; underneath whose arm
An envious thrust from Tybalt hit the life
Of stout Mercutio, and then Tybalt fled;
But by and by comes back to Romeo,
Who had but newly entertained revenge,
And to't they go like lightning; for, ere I
Could draw to part them, was stout Tybalt slain;
And, as he fell, did Romeo turn and fly.
This is the truth, or let Benvolio die.

Lady Capulet. He is a kinsman to the Montague;
Affection makes him false, he speaks not true.
Some twenty of them fought in this black strife,
And all those twenty could but kill one life.
I beg for justice, which thou, Prince, must give.
Romeo slew Tybalt; Romeo must not live.

Prince. Romeo slew him; he slew Mercutio.
Who now the price of his dear blood doth owe?

Capulet. Not Romeo, Prince; he was Mercutio's friend;
His fault concludes but what the law should end,
The life of Tybalt.

Prince.   And for that offense
Immediately we do exile him hence.
I have an interest in your hate's proceeding,
My blood for your rude brawls doth lie a-bleeding;
But I'll amerce you with so strong a fine
That you shall all repent the loss of mine.
I will be deaf to pleading and excuses;
Nor tears nor prayers shall purchase out abuses.
Therefore use none. Let Romeo hence in haste,
Else, when he is found, that hour is his last.
Bear hence this body and attend our will.
Mercy but murders, pardoning those that kill.

   [*Exit with others*]

SCENE II
CAPULET'S ORCHARD

[Enter Juliet alone]

Juliet.   Gallop apace, you fiery-footed steeds,

Towards Phoebus' lodging! Such a wagoner

As Phaëton would whip you to the west

And bring in cloudy night immediately.

Spread thy close curtain, love-performing night,

That runaways' eyes may wink, and Romeo

Leap to these arms untalked of and unseen.

Lovers can see to do their amorous rites,

And by their own beauties; or, if love be blind,

It best agrees with night. Come, civil night,

Thou sober-suited matron all in black,

And learn me how to lose a winning match,

Played for a pair of stainless maidenhoods.

Hood my unmanned blood, bating in my cheeks,

With thy black mantle till strange love grow bold,

Think true love acted simple modesty.

Come, night; come, Romeo; come, thou day in night;

For thou wilt lie upon the wings of night

Whiter than new snow upon a raven's back.

Come, gentle night; come, loving, black-browed night;

Give me my Romeo; and, when I shall die,

Take him and cut him out in little stars,

And he will make the face of heaven so fine

That all the world will be in love with night

And pay no worship to the garish sun.

O, I have bought the mansion of a love,

But not possessed it; and though I am sold,

Not yet enjoyed. So tedious is this day

As is the night before some festival

To an impatient child that hath new robes

And may not wear them. O, here comes my nurse,

    [Enter Nurse, with cords]

And she brings news; and every tongue that speaks

But Romeo's name speaks heavenly eloquence.

Now, nurse, what news? What hast thou there, the cords

That Romeo bid thee fetch?

Nurse.	Ay, ay, the cords.
Juliet.	Ay me! What news? Why dost thou wring thy hands?
Nurse.	Ah, weraday! He's dead, he's dead, he's dead!
	We are undone, lady, we are undone!
	Alack the day! He's gone, he's killed, he's dead!
Juliet.	Can heaven be so envious?
Nurse.	Romeo can,
	Though heaven cannot. O Romeo, Romeo!
	Who ever would have thought it? Romeo!
Juliet.	What devil art thou that dost torment me thus?
	This torture should be roared in dismal hell.
	Hath Romeo slain himself? Say thou but "Ay,"
	And that bare vowel "I" shall poison more
	Than the death-darting eye of cockatrice.
	I am not I, if there be such an "Ay,"
	Or those eyes' shot that makes thee answer "Ay."
	If he be slain, say "Ay"; or if not, "No."
	Brief sounds determine of my weal or woe.

Nurse. I saw the wound, I saw it with mine eyes,
(God save the mark!) here on his manly breast.
A piteous corse, a bloody piteous corse;
Pale, pale as ashes, all bedaubed in blood,
All in gore-blood. I sounded at the sight.

Juliet. O, break, my heart! Poor bankrout, break at once!
To prison, eyes; ne'er look on liberty!
Vile earth, to earth resign; end motion here,
And thou and Romeo press one heavy bier!

Nurse. O Tybalt, Tybalt, the best friend I had!
O courteous Tybalt! Honest gentleman!
That ever I should live to see thee dead!

Juliet. What storm is this that blows so contrary?
Is Romeo slaught'red, and is Tybalt dead?
My dearest cousin, and my dearer lord?
Then, dreadful trumpet, sound the general doom!
For who is living, if those two are gone?

Nurse. Tybalt is gone, and Romeo banishèd;
Romeo that killed him, he is banishèd.

Juliet.	O God! Did Romeo's hand shed Tybalt's blood?
Nurse.	It did, it did! Alas the day, it did!
Juliet.	O serpent heart, hid with a flow'ring face!
	Did ever dragon keep so fair a cave?
	Beautiful tyrant! Fiend angelical!
	Dove-feathered raven! Wolvish-ravening lamb!
	Despisèd substance of divinest show!
	Just opposite to what thou justly seem'st—
	A damnèd saint, an honorable villain!
	O nature, what hadst thou to do in hell
	When thou didst bower the spirit of a fiend
	In mortal paradise of such sweet flesh?
	Was ever book containing such vile matter
	So fairly bound? O, that deceit should dwell
	In such a gorgeous palace!
Nurse.	There's no trust,
	No faith, no honesty in men; all perjured,
	All forsworn, all naught, all dissemblers.
	Ah, where's my man? Give me some *aqua vitae.*
	These griefs, these woes, these sorrows make me old.
	Shame come to Romeo!

Juliet.   Blistered be thy tongue
For such a wish! He was not born to shame.
Upon his brow shame is ashamed to sit;
For 'tis a throne where honor may be crowned
Sole monarch of the universal earth.
O, what a beast was I to chide at him!

Nurse. Will you speak well of him that killed your cousin?

Juliet. Shall I speak ill of him that is my husband?
Ah, poor my lord, what tongue shall smooth thy name
When I, thy three-hours wife, have mangled it?
But wherefore, villain, didst thou kill my cousin?
That villain cousin would have killed my husband.
Back, foolish tears, back to your native spring!
Your tributary drops belong to woe,
Which you, mistaking, offer up to joy.
My husband lives, that Tybalt would have slain;
And Tybalt's dead, that would have slain my husband.
All this is comfort; wherefore weep I then?
Some word there was, worser than Tybalt's death,
That murd'red me. I would forget it fain;
But O, it presses to my memory

Like damnèd guilty deeds to sinners' minds!
"Tybalt is dead, and Romeo—banishèd."
That "banishèd," that one word "banishèd,"
Hath slain ten thousand Tybalts. Tybalt's death
Was woe enough, if it had ended there;
Or, if sour woe delights in fellowship
And needly will be ranked with other griefs,
Why followed not, when she said "Tybalt's dead,"
Thy father, or thy mother, nay, or both,
Which modern lamentation might have moved?
But with a rearward following Tybalt's death,
"Romeo is banishèd"—to speak that word
Is father, mother, Tybalt, Romeo, Juliet,
All slain, all dead. "Romeo is banishèd"—
There is no end, no limit, measure, bound,
In that word's death; no words can that woe sound.
Where is my father and my mother, nurse?

Nurse. Weeping and wailing over Tybalt's corse.
Will you go to them? I will bring you thither.

Juliet. Wash they his wounds with tears? Mine shall be spent,
When theirs are dry, for Romeo's banishment.
Take up those cords. Poor ropes, you are beguiled,
Both you and I, for Romeo is exiled.
He made you for a highway to my bed;
But I, a maid, die maiden-widowèd.
Come, cords; come, nurse. I'll to my wedding bed;
And death, not Romeo, take my maidenhead!

Nurse. Hie to your chamber. I'll find Romeo
To comfort you. I wot well where he is.
Hark ye, your Romeo will be here at night.
I'll to him; he is hid at Lawrence' cell.

Juliet. O, find him! Give this ring to my true knight
And bid him come to take his last farewell.
[*Exit with Nurse*]

[Enter Friar Lawrence]

Friar.   Romeo, come forth; come forth, thou fearful man.

Affliction is enamored of thy parts,

And thou art wedded to calamity.

[Enter Romeo]

Romeo.   Father, what news? What is the Prince's doom?

What sorrow craves acquaintance at my hand

That I yet know not?

Friar.   Too familiar

Is my dear son with such sour company.

I bring thee tidings of the Prince's doom.

Romeo.   What less than doomsday is the Prince's doom?

Friar.   A gentler judgment vanished from his lips—

Not body's death, but body's banishment.

Romeo.   Ha, banishment? Be merciful, say "death";

For exile hath more terror in his look,

Much more than death. Do not say "banishment."

Friar. Here from Verona art thou banishèd.
Be patient, for the world is broad and wide.

Romeo. There is no world without Verona walls,
But purgatory, torture, hell itself.
Hence banishèd is banished from the world,
And world's exile is death. Then "banishèd"
Is death mistermed. Calling death "banishèd,"
Thou cut'st my head off with a golden ax
And smilest upon the stroke that murders me.

Friar. O deadly sin! O rude unthankfulness!
Thy fault our law calls death; but the kind Prince,
Taking thy part, hath rushed aside the law,
And turned that black word "death" to "banishment."
This is dear mercy, and thou seest it not.

Romeo. 'Tis torture, and not mercy. Heaven is here,
Where Juliet lives; and every cat and dog
And little mouse, every unworthy thing,
Live here in heaven and may look on her;
But Romeo may not. More validity,
More honorable state, more courtship lives
In carrion flies than Romeo. They may seize
On the white wonder of dear Juliet's hand
And steal immortal blessing from her lips,
Who, even in pure and vestal modesty,
Still blush, as thinking their own kisses sin;
But Romeo may not, he is banishèd.
Flies may do this but I from this must fly;
They are freemen, but I am banishèd.
And sayest thou yet that exile is not death?
Hadst thou no poison mixed, no sharp-ground knife,
No sudden mean of death, though ne'er so mean,
But "banishèd" to kill me—"banishèd"?
O friar, the damnèd use that word in hell;
Howling attends it! How hast thou the heart,
Being a devine, a ghostly confessor,
A sin-absolver, and my friend professed,
To mangle me with that word "banishèd"?

Friar.   Thou fond mad man, hear me a little speak.

Romeo.   O, thou wilt speak again of banishment.

Friar.   I'll give thee armor to keep off that word;
Adversity's sweet milk, philosophy,
To comfort thee, though thou art banishèd.

Romeo.   Yet "banishèd"? Hang up philosophy!
Unless philosophy can make a Juliet,
Displant a town, reverse a prince's doom,
It helps not, it prevails not. Talk no more.

Friar.   O, then I see that madmen have no ears.

Romeo.   How should they, when that wise men have no eyes?

Friar.   Let me dispute with thee of thy estate.

Romeo.   Thou canst not speak of that thou dost not feel.
Wert thou as young as I, Juliet thy love,
An hour but married, Tybalt murderèd,
Doting like me, and like me banishèd,
Then mightst thou speak, then mightst thou tear thy hair,
And fall upon the ground, as I do now,
Taking the measure of an unmade grave.

   [*Enter Nurse and knock*]

Friar. Arise, one knocks. Good Romeo, hide thyself.

Romeo. Not I; unless the breath of heartsick groans
Mistlike infold me from the search of eyes.
    [*Knock*]

Friar. Hark, how they knock! Who's there? Romeo, arise;
Thou wilt be taken.—Stay awhile!—Stand up;
    [*Knock*]
Run to my study.—By and by!—God's will,
What simpleness is this.—I come, I come!
    [*Knock*]
Who knocks so hard? Whence come you? What's your will?
    [*Enter Nurse*]

Nurse. Let me come in, and you shall know my errand.
I come from Lady Juliet.

Friar.   Welcome then.

Nurse. O holy friar, O, tell me, holy friar,
Where is my lady's lord, where's Romeo?

Friar. There on the ground, with his own tears made drunk.

Nurse.	O, he is even in my mistress' case,
	Just in her case! O woeful sympathy!
	Piteous predicament! Even so lies she,
	Blubb'ring and weeping, weeping and blubb'ring.
	Stand up, stand up! Stand, and you be a man.
	For Juliet's sake, for her sake, rise and stand!
	Why should you fall into so deep an O?
Romeo.	[*Rises*] Nurse—
Nurse.	Ah sir, ah sir! Death's the end of all.
Romeo.	Spakest thou of Juliet? How is it with her?
	Doth not she think me an old murderer,
	Now I have stained the childhood of our joy
	With blood removed but little from her own?
	Where is she? And how doth she! And what says
	My concealed lady to our canceled love?
Nurse.	O, she says nothing, sir, but weeps and weeps;
	And now falls on her bed, and then starts up,
	And Tybalt calls; and then on Romeo cries,
	And then down falls again.

Romeo. As if that name,
Shot from the deadly level of a gun,
Did murder her; as that name's cursèd hand
Murdered her kinsman. O, tell me, friar, tell me,
In what vile part of this anatomy
Doth my name lodge? Tell me, that I may sack
The hateful mansion.

    [He offers to stab himself, and the
    Nurse snatches the dagger away]

Friar. Hold thy desperate hand.
Art thou a man? Thy form cries out thou art;
Thy tears are womanish, thy wild acts denote
The unreasonable fury of a beast.
Unseemly woman in a seeming man!
And ill-beseeming beast in seeming both!
Thou hast amazed me. By my holy order,
I thought thy disposition better tempered.
Hast thou slain Tybalt? Wilt thou slay thyself?
And slay thy lady that in thy life lives,
By doing damnèd hate upon thyself?
Why railest thou on thy birth, the heaven, and earth?
Since birth and heaven and earth, all three do meet
In thee at once; which thou at once wouldst lose.

Fie, fie, thou shamest thy shape, thy love, thy wit,
Which, like a usurer, abound'st in all,
And usest none in that true use indeed
Which should bedeck thy shape, thy love, thy wit.
Thy noble shape is but a form of wax,
Digressing from the valor of a man;
Thy dear love sworn but hollow perjury,
Killing that love which thou hast vowed to cherish;
Thy wit, that ornament to shape and love,
Misshapen in the conduct of them both,
Like powder in a skilless soldier's flask,
Is set afire by thine own ignorance,
And thou dismemb'red with thine own defense.
What, rouse thee, man! Thy Juliet is alive,
For whose dear sake thou wast but lately dead.
There art thou happy. Tybalt would kill thee,
But thou slewest Tybalt. There art thou happy.
The law, that threat'ned death, becomes thy friend
And turns it to exile. There art thou happy.
A pack of blessings light upon thy back;
Happiness courts thee in her best array;
But, like a misbehaved and sullen wench,

Thou puts up thy fortune and thy love.
Take heed, take heed, for such die miserable.
Go get thee to thy love, as was decreed,
Ascend her chamber, hence and comfort her.
But look thou stay not till the watch be set,
For then thou canst not pass to Mantua,
Where thou shalt live till we can find a time
To blaze your marriage, reconcile your friends,
Beg pardon of the Prince, and call thee back
With twenty hundred thousand times more joy
Than thou went'st forth in lamentation.
Go before, nurse. Commend me to thy lady,
And bid her hasten all the house to bed,
Which heavy sorrow makes them apt unto.
Romeo is coming.

Nurse. O Lord, I could have stayed here all the night
To hear good counsel. O, what learning is!
My lord, I'll tell my lady you will come.

Romeo. Do so, and bid my sweet prepare to chide.
  [*Nurse offers to go in and turns again*]

Nurse. Here, sir, a ring she bid me give you, sir.
Hie you, make haste, for it grows very late.
  [*Exit*]

Romeo. How well my comfort is revived by this!

Friar. Go hence; good night; and here stands all your state:
Either be gone before the watch be set,
Or by the break of day disguised from hence.
Sojourn in Mantua. I'll find out your man,
And he shall signify from time to time
Every good hap to you that chances here.
Give me thy hand. 'Tis late. Farewell; good night.

Romeo. But that a joy past joy calls out on me,
It were a grief so brief to part with thee.
Farewell.

[*Exeunt*]

[Enter old Capulet, his Wife, and Paris]

Capulet. Things have fall'n out, sir, so unluckily
That we have had no time to move our daughter.
Look you, she loved her kinsman Tybalt dearly,
And so did I. Well, we were born to die.
'Tis very late; she'll not come down tonight.
I promise you, but for your company,
I would have been abed an hour ago.

Paris. These times of woe afford no times to woo.
Madam, good night. Commend me to your daughter.

Lady. I will, and know her mind early tomorrow;
Tonight she's mewed up to her heaviness.

Capulet. Sir Paris, I will make a desperate tender
Of my child's love. I think she will be ruled
In all respects by me; nay more, I doubt it not.
Wife, go you to her ere you go to bed;
Acquaint her here of my son Paris' love
And bid her (mark you me?) on Wednesday next—
But soft! What day is this?

Paris.	Monday, my lord.
Capulet.	Monday! Ha, ha! Well, Wednesday is too soon.
	A Thursday let it be—a Thursday, tell her,
	She shall be married to this noble earl.
	Will you be ready? Do you like this haste?
	We'll keep no great ado—a friend or two;
	For hark you, Tybalt being slain so late,
	It may be thought we held him carelessly,
	Being our kinsman, if we revel much.
	Therefore we'll have some half a dozen friends,
	And there an end. But what say you to Thursday?
Paris.	My lord, I would that Thursday were tomorrow.
Capulet.	Well, get you gone. A Thursday be it then.
	Go you to Juliet ere you go to bed;
	Prepare her, wife, against this wedding day.
	Farewell, my lord.—Light to my chamber, ho!
	Afore me, it is so very late
	That we may call it early by and by.
	Good night.

[*Exeunt*]

SCENE V
CAPULET'S ORCHARD

[*Enter Romeo and Juliet aloft*]

Juliet. Wilt thou be gone? It is not yet near day.
It was the nightingale, and not the lark,
That pierced the fearful hollow of thine ear.
Nightly she sings on yond pomegranate tree.
Believe me, love, it was the nightingale.

Romeo. It was the lark, the herald of the morn;
No nightingale. Look, love, what envious streaks
Do lace the severing clouds in yonder East.
Night's candles are burnt out, and jocund day
Stands tiptoe on the misty mountaintops.
I must be gone and live, or stay and die.

Juliet. Yond light is not daylight; I know it, I.
It is some meteor that the sun exhales
To be to thee this night a torchbearer
And light thee on thy way to Mantua.
Therefore stay yet; thou need'st not to be gone.

LADY CAPULET

Romeo. Let me be ta'en, let me be put to death.
I am content, so thou wilt have it so.
I'll say yon gray is not the morning's eye,
'Tis but the pale reflex of Cynthia's brow;
Nor that is not the lark whose notes do beat
The vaulty heaven so high above our heads.
I have more care to stay than will to go.
Come, death, and welcome! Juliet wills it so.
How is't, my soul? Let's talk; it is not day.

Juliet. It is, it is! Hie hence, be gone, away!
It is the lark that sings so out of tune,
Straining harsh discords and unpleasing sharps.
Some say the lark makes sweet division;
This doth not so, for she divideth us.
Some say the lark and loathèd toad change eyes;
O, now I would they had changed voices too,
Since arm from arm that voice doth us affray,
Hunting thee hence with hunt's-up to the day.
O, now be gone! More light and light it grows.

Romeo. More light and light—more dark and dark our woes.
    [Enter Nurse]
Nurse. Madam!
Juliet. Nurse?
Nurse. Your lady mother is coming to your chamber.
    The day is broke; be wary, look about.
    [Exit]
Juliet. Then, window, let day in, and let life out.
Romeo. Farewell, farewell! One kiss, and I'll descend.
    [He goes down]
Juliet. Art thou gone so, love-lord, ay husband-friend?
    I must hear from thee every day in the hour,
    For in a minute there are many days.
    O, by this count I shall be much in years
    Ere I again behold my Romeo!
Romeo. Farewell!
    I will omit no opportunity
    That may convey my greetings, love, to thee.
Juliet. O, think'st thou we shall ever meet again?
Romeo. I doubt it not; and all these woes shall serve
    For sweet discourses in our times to come.

Juliet.	O God, I have an ill-divining soul!
	Methinks I see thee, now thou art so low,
	As one dead in the bottom of a tomb.
	Either my eyesight fails, or thou lookest pale.
Romeo.	And trust me, love, in my eye so do you.
	Dry sorrow drinks our blood. Adieu, adieu!
	[*Exit*]
Juliet.	O Fortune, Fortune! All men call thee fickle.
	If thou art fickle, what dost thou with him
	That is renowned for faith? Be fickle, Fortune,
	For then I hope thou wilt not keep him long
	But send him back.
	[*Enter Mother*]
Lady Capulet.	Ho, daughter! Are you up?
Juliet.	Who is't that calls? It is my lady mother.
	Is she not down so late, or up so early?
	What unaccustomed cause procures her hither?

Lady Capulet.	Why, how now, Juliet?
Juliet.	Madam, I am not well.
Lady Capulet.	Evermore weeping for your cousin's death?
	What, wilt thou wash him from his grave with tears?
	And if thou couldst, thou couldst not make him live.
	Therefore have done. Some grief shows much of love;
	But much of grief shows still some want of wit.
Juliet.	Yet let me weep for such a feeling loss.
Lady Capulet.	So shall you feel the loss, but not the friend
	Which you weep for.
Juliet.	Feeling so the loss,
	I cannot choose but ever weep the friend.
Lady Capulet.	Well, girl, thou weep'st not so much for his death
	As that the villain lives which slaughtered him.
Juliet.	What villain, madam?
Lady Capulet.	That same villain Romeo.
Juliet.	[*Aside*] Villain and he be many miles asunder.—
	God pardon him! I do, with all my heart;
	And yet no man like he doth grieve my heart.

Lady Capulet.	That is because the traitor murderer lives.
Juliet.	Ay, madam, from the reach of these my hands.
	Would none but I might venge my cousin's death!
Lady Capulet.	We will have vengeance for it, fear thou not.
	Then weep no more. I'll send to one in Mantua,
	Where that same banished runagate doth live,
	Shall give him such an unaccustomed dram
	That he shall soon keep Tybalt company;
	And then I hope thou wilt be satisfied.
Juliet.	Indeed I never shall be satisfied
	With Romeo till I behold him—dead—
	Is my poor heart so for a kinsman vexed.
	Madam, if you could find out but a man
	To bear a poison, I would temper it;
	That Romeo should, upon receipt thereof,
	Soon sleep in quiet. O, how my heart abhors
	To hear him named and cannot come to him,
	To wreak the love I bore my cousin
	Upon his body that hath slaughtered him!

Lady Capulet.	Find thou the means, and I'll find such a man.
	But now I'll tell thee joyful tidings, girl.
Juliet.	And joy comes well in such a needy time.
	What are they, beseech your ladyship?
Lady Capulet.	Well, well, thou hast a careful father, child;
	One who, to put thee from thy heaviness,
	Hath sorted out a sudden day of joy
	That thou expects not nor I looked not for.
Juliet.	Madam, in happy time! What day is that?
Lady Capulet.	Marry, my child, early next Thursday morn
	The gallant, young, and noble gentleman,
	The County Paris, at Saint Peter's Church,
	Shall happily make thee there a joyful bride.
Juliet.	Now by Saint Peter's Church, and Peter too,
	He shall not make me there a joyful bride!
	I wonder at this haste, that I must wed
	Ere he that should be husband comes to woo.
	I pray you tell my lord and father, madam,
	I will not marry yet; and when I do, I swear
	It shall be Romeo, whom you know I hate,
	Rather than Paris. These are news indeed!

Lady Capulet. Here comes your father. Tell him so yourself,
And see how he will take it at your hands.
            [Enter Capulet and Nurse]
Capulet. When the sun sets the earth doth drizzle dew,
But for the sunset of my brother's son
It rains downright.
How now? A conduit, girl? What, still in tears?
Evermore show'ring? In one little body
Thou counterfeits a bark, a sea, a wind:
For still thy eyes, which I may call the sea,
Do ebb and flow with tears; the bark thy body is,
Sailing in this salt flood; the winds, thy sighs,
Who, raging with thy tears and they with them,
Without a sudden calm will overset
Thy tempest-tossèd body. How now, wife?
Have you delivered to her our decree?
Lady Capulet. Ay, sir; but she will none, she gives you thanks.
I would the fool were married to her grave!

Capulet. Soft! Take me with you, take me with you, wife.
How? Will she none? Doth she not give us thanks?
Is she not proud? Doth she not count her blest,
Unworthy as she is, that we have wrought
So worthy a gentleman to be her bride?

Juliet. Not proud you have, but thankful that you have.
Proud can I never be of what I hate,
But thankful even for hate that is meant love.

Capulet. How, how, how, how, chopped-logic? What is this?
"Proud"—and "I thank you"—and "I thank you not"—
And yet "not proud"? Mistress minion you,
Thank me no thankings, nor proud me no prouds,
But fettle your fine joints 'gainst Thursday next
To go with Paris to Saint Peter's Church,
Or I will drag thee on a hurdle thither.
Out, you greensickness carrion! Out, you baggage!
You tallow-face!

Lady Capulet.	Fie, fie! What, are you mad?
Juliet.	Good father, I beseech you on my knees,
	Hear me with patience but to speak a word.
Capulet.	Hang thee, young baggage! Disobedient wretch!
	I tell thee what—get thee to church a Thursday
	Or never after look me in the face.
	Speak not, reply not, do not answer me!
	My fingers itch. Wife, we scarce thought us blest
	That God had lent us but this only child;
	But now I see this one is one too much,
	And that we have a curse in having her.
	Out on her, hilding!
Nurse.	God in heaven bless her!
	You are to blame, my lord, to rate her so.
Capulet.	And why, my Lady Wisdom? Hold your tongue,
	Good Prudence. Smatter with your gossips, go!
Nurse.	I speak no treason.
Capulet.	O, God-i-god-en!
Nurse.	May not one speak?
Capulet.	Peace, you mumbling fool!
	Utter your gravity o'er a gossip's bowl,
	For here we need it not.

Lady Capulet.   You are too hot.

Capulet.   God's bread! It makes me mad.

Day, night; hour, tide, time; work, play;

Alone, in company; still my care hath been

To have her matched; and having now provided

A gentleman of noble parentage,

Of fair demesnes, youthful, and nobly trained,

Stuffed, as they say, with honorable parts,

Proportioned as one's thought would wish a man—

And then to have a wretched puling fool,

A whining mammet, in her fortune's tender,

To answer "I'll not wed, I cannot love;

I am too young, I pray you pardon me"!

But, and you will not wed, I'll pardon you!

Graze where you will, you shall not house with me.

Look to't, think on't; I do not use to jest.

Thursday is near; lay hand on heart, advise:

And you be mine, I'll give you to my friend;

And you be not, hang, beg, starve, die in the streets,

For, by my soul, I'll ne'er acknowledge thee,

Nor what is mine shall never do thee good.

Trust to't. Bethink you. I'll not be forsworn.

    [Exit]

Juliet. Is there no pity sitting in the clouds
That sees into the bottom of my grief?
O sweet my mother, cast me not away!
Delay this marriage for a month, a week;
Or if you do not, make the bridal bed
In that dim monument where Tybalt lies.

Lady Capulet. Talk not to me, for I'll not speak a word.
Do as thou wilt, for I have done with thee.
                [*Exit*]

Juliet. O God!—O nurse, how shall this be prevented?
My husband is on earth, my faith in heaven.
How shall that faith return again to earth
Unless that husband send it me from heaven
By leaving earth? Comfort me, counsel me.
Alack, alack, that heaven should practice stratagems
Upon so soft a subject as myself!
What say'st thou? Hast thou not a word of joy?
Some comfort, nurse.

Nurse.	Faith, here it is.
	Romeo is banished; and all the world to nothing
	That he dares ne'er come back to challenge you;
	Or if he do, it needs must be by stealth.
	Then, since the case so stands as now it doth,
	I think it best you married with the County.
	O, he's a lovely gentleman!
	Romeo's a dishclout to him. An eagle, madam,
	Hath not so green, so quick, so fair an eye
	As Paris hath. Beshrew my very heart,
	I think you are happy in this second match,
	For it excels your first; or if it did not,
	Your first is dead—or 'twere as good he were
	As living here and you no use of him.
Juliet.	Speak'st thou from thy heart?
Nurse.	And from my soul too; else beshrew them both.
Juliet.	Amen!
Nurse.	What?
Juliet.	Well, thou hast comforted me marvelous much.
	Go in; and tell my lady I am gone,
	Having displeased my father, to Lawrence' cell,
	To make confession and to be absolved.

Nurse. Marry, I will; and this is wisely done.

      [Exit]

Juliet. Ancient damnation! O most wicked fiend!

      Is it more sin to wish me thus forsworn,

      Or to dispraise my lord with that same tongue

      Which she hath praised him with above compare

      So many thousand times? Go, counselor!

      Thou and my bosom henceforth shall be twain.

      I'll to the friar to know his remedy.

      If all else fail, myself have power to die.

      [Exit]

ACT FOUR

SCENE I
FRIAR LAWRENCE'S CELL

[*Enter Friar Lawrence and County Paris*]

Friar.   On Thursday, sir? The time is very short.

Paris.   My father Capulet will have it so,
And I am nothing slow to slack his haste.

Friar.   You say you do not know the lady's mind.
Uneven is the course; I like it not.

Paris.   Immoderately she weeps for Tybalt's death,
And therefore have I little talked of love;
For Venus smiles not in a house of tears.
Now, sir, her father counts it dangerous
That she do give her sorrow so much sway,
And in his wisdom hastes our marriage
To stop the inundation of her tears,
Which, too much minded by herself alone,
May be put from her by society.
Now do you know the reason of this haste.

Friar.	[*Aside*] I would I knew not why it should be slowed.—
	Look, sir, here comes the lady toward my cell.
	[*Enter Juliet*]
Paris.	Happily met, my lady and my wife!
Juliet.	That may be, sir, when I may be a wife.
Paris.	That "may be" must be, love, on Thursday next.
Juliet.	What must be shall be.
Friar.	That's a certain text.
Paris.	Come you to make confession to this father?
Juliet.	To answer that, I should confess to you.
Paris.	Do not deny to him that you love me.
Juliet.	I will confess to you that I love him.
Paris.	So will ye, I am sure, that you love me.
Juliet.	If I do so, it will be of more price,
	Being spoke behind your back, than to your face.
Paris.	Poor soul, thy face is much abused with tears.
Juliet.	The tears have got small victory by that,
	For it was bad enough before their spite.
Paris.	Thou wrong'st it more than tears with that report.

Juliet. That is no slander, sir, which is a truth;

And what I spake, I spake it to my face.

Paris. Thy face is mine, and thou hast sland'red it.

Juliet. It may be so, for it is not mine own.

Are you at leisure, holy father, now,

Or shall I come to you at evening mass?

Friar. My leisure serves me, pensive daughter, now.

My lord, we must entreat the time alone.

Paris. God shield I should disturb devotion!

Juliet, on Thursday early will I rouse ye.

Till then, adieu, and keep this holy kiss.

   [*Exit*]

Juliet. O, shut the door, and when thou hast done so,

Come weep with me—past hope, past care, past help!

Friar. O Juliet, I already know thy grief;

It strains me past the compass of my wits.

I hear thou must, and nothing may prorogue it,

On Thursday next be married to this County.

Juliet. Tell me not, friar, that thou hearest of this,
Unless thou tell me how I may prevent it.
If in thy wisdom thou canst give no help,
Do thou but call my resolution wise
And with this knife I'll help it presently.
God joined my heart and Romeo's, thou our hands;
And ere this hand, by thee to Romeo's sealed,
Shall be the label to another deed,
Or my true heart with treacherous revolt
Turn to another, this shall slay them both.
Therefore, out of thy long-experienced time,
Give me some present counsel; or, behold,
'Twixt my extremes and me this bloody knife
Shall play the umpire, arbitrating that
Which the commission of thy years and art
Could to no issue of true honor bring.
Be not so long to speak. I long to die
If what thou speak'st speak not of remedy.

Friar. Hold, daughter. I do spy a kind of hope,
Which craves as desperate an execution
As that is desperate which we would prevent.
If, rather than to marry County Paris,
Thou hast the strength of will to slay thyself,
Then is it likely thou wilt undertake
A thing like death to chide away this shame,
That cop'st with death himself to scape from it;
And, if thou darest, I'll give thee remedy.

Juliet. O, bid me leap, rather than marry Paris,
From off the battlements of any tower,
Or walk in thievish ways, or bid me lurk
Where serpents are; chain me with roaring bears,
Or hide me nightly in a charnel house,
O'ercovered quite with dead men's rattling bones,
With reeky shanks and yellow chapless skulls;
Or bid me go into a new-made grave
And hide me with a dead man in his shroud—
Things that, to hear them told, have made me tremble—
And I will do it without fear or doubt,
To live an unstained wife to my sweet love.

Friar. Hold, then. Go home, be merry, give consent
To marry Paris. Wednesday is tomorrow.
Tomorrow night look that thou lie alone;
Let not the nurse lie with thee in thy chamber.
Take thou this vial, being then in bed,
And this distilling liquor drink thou off;
When presently through all thy veins shall run
A cold and drowsy humor; for no pulse
Shall keep his native progress, but surcease;
No warmth, no breath, shall testify thou livest;
The roses in thy lips and cheeks shall fade
To wanny ashes, thy eyes' windows fall
Like death when he shuts up the day of life;
Each part, deprived of supple government,
Shall, stiff and stark and cold, appear like death;
And in this borrowed likeness of shrunk death
Thou shalt continue two-and-forty hours,
And then awake as from a pleasant sleep.

Now, when the bridegroom in the morning comes
To rouse thee from thy bed, there art thou dead.
Then, as the manner of our country is,
In thy best robes uncovered on the bier
Thou shalt be borne to that same ancient vault
Where all the kindred of the Capulets lie.
In the meantime, against thou shalt awake,
Shall Romeo by my letters know our drift;
And hither shall he come; and he and I
Will watch thy waking, and that very night
Shall Romeo bear thee hence to Mantua.
And this shall free thee from this present shame,
If no inconstant toy nor womanish fear
Abate thy valor in the acting it.

Juliet. Give me, give me! O, tell not me of fear!

Friar. Hold! Get you gone, be strong and prosperous
In this resolve. I'll send a friar with speed
To Mantua, with my letters to thy lord.

Juliet. Love give me strength, and strength shall help afford.
Farewell, dear father.
    [*Exit with Friar*]

SCENE II
HALL IN CAPULET'S HOUSE

[*Enter Father Capulet, Mother,*
Nurse, and several Servingmen]

Capulet. So many guests invite as here are writ.
    [*Exit a Servingman*]
Sirrah, go hire me twenty cunning cooks.

Servingman. You shall have none ill, sir; for I'll try if they
can lick their fingers.

Capulet. How canst thou try them so?

Servingman. Marry, sir, 'tis an ill cook that cannot lick his
own fingers. Therefore he that cannot lick his
fingers goes not with me.

Capulet. Go, begone.
    [*Exit a Servingman*]
We shall be much unfurnished for this time.
What, is my daughter gone to Friar Lawrence?

Nurse.	Ay, forsooth.
Capulet.	Well, he may chance to do some good on her.
	A peevish self-willed harlotry it is.
	[*Enter Juliet*]
Nurse.	See where she comes from shrift with merry look.
Capulet.	How now, my headstrong? Where have you
	been gadding?
Juliet.	Where I have learnt me to repent the sin
	Of disobedient opposition
	To you and your behests, and am enjoined
	By holy Lawrence to fall prostrate here
	To beg your pardon. Pardon, I beseech you!
	Henceforward I am ever ruled by you.
Capulet.	Send for the County. Go tell him of this.
	I'll have this knot knit up tomorrow morning.
Juliet.	I met the youthful lord at Lawrence' cell
	And gave him what becomèd love I might,
	Not stepping o'er the bounds of modesty.
Capulet.	Why, I am glad on't. This is well. Stand up.
	This is as't should be. Let me see the County.
	Ay, marry, go, I say, and fetch him hither.
	Now, afore God, this reverend holy friar,
	All our whole city is much bound to him.

Juliet.	Nurse, will you go with me into my closet
	To help me sort such needful ornaments
	As you think fit to furnish me tomorrow?
Lady Capulet.	No, not till Thursday. There is time enough.
Capulet.	Go, nurse, go with her. We'll to church tomorrow.

[*Exeunt Juliet and Nurse*]

Lady Capulet.	We shall be short in our provision.
	'Tis now near night.
Capulet.	Tush, I will stir about,
	And all things shall be well, I warrant thee, wife.
	Go thou to Juliet, help to deck up her.
	I'll not to bed tonight; let me alone.
	I'll play the housewife for this once. What, ho!
	They are all forth; well, I will walk myself
	To County Paris, to prepare up him
	Against tomorrow. My heart is wondrous light,
	Since this same wayward girl is so reclaimed.

[*Exit with Mother*]

SCENE III
JULIET'S CHAMBER

[*Enter Juliet and Nurse*]

Juliet. Ay, those attires are best; but, gentle nurse,
I pray thee leave me to myself tonight;
For I have need of many orisons
To move the heavens to smile upon my state,
Which, well thou knowest, is cross and full of sin.
[*Enter Mother*]

Lady Capulet. What, are you busy, ho? Need you my help?

Juliet. No, madam; we have culled such necessaries
As are behoveful for our state tomorrow.
So please you, let me now be left alone,
And let the nurse this night sit up with you;
For I am sure you have your hands full all
In this so sudden business.

Lady Capulet.   Good night.
Get thee to bed, and rest; for thou hast need.
[*Exeunt Mother and Nurse*]

Juliet. Farewell! God knows when we shall meet again.
I have a faint cold fear thrills through my veins
That almost freezes up the heat of life.
I'll call them back again to comfort me.
Nurse!—What should she do here?
My dismal scene I needs must act alone.
Come, vial.
What if this mixture do not work at all?
Shall I be married then tomorrow morning?
No, no! This shall forbid it. Lie thou there.

    [*Lays down a dagger*]

What if it be a poison which the friar
Subtly hath minist'red to have me dead,
Lest in this marriage he should be dishonored
Because he married me before to Romeo?
I fear it is; and yet methinks it should not,
For he hath still been tried a holy man.
How if, when I am laid into the tomb,
I wake before the time that Romeo
Come to redeem me? There's a fearful point!
Shall I not then be stifled in the vault,
To whose foul mouth no healthsome air breathes in,
And there die strangled ere my Romeo comes?

LADY MONTAGUE

Or, if I live, is it not very like
The horrible conceit of death and night,
Together with the terror of the place—
As in a vault, an ancient receptacle
Where for this many hundred years the bones
Of all my buried ancestors are packed;
Where bloody Tybalt, yet but green in earth,
Lies fest'ring in his shroud; where, as they say,
At some hours in the night spirits resort—
Alack, alack, is it not like that I,
So early waking—what with loathsome smells,
And shrieks like mandrakes torn out of the earth,
That living mortals, hearing them, run mad—
O, if I wake, shall I not be distraught,
Environed with all these hideous fears,
And madly play with my forefathers' joints,
And pluck the mangled Tybalt from his shroud,
And, in this rage, with some great kinsman's bone
As with a club dash out my desp'rate brains?
O, look! Methinks I see my cousin's ghost
Seeking out Romeo, that did spit his body
Upon a rapier's point. Stay, Tybalt, stay!
Romeo, Romeo, Romeo, I drink to thee.
    [She falls upon her bed within the curtains]

SCENE IV
HALL IN CAPULET'S HOUSE

[Enter Lady of the House and Nurse]

Lady Capulet.   Hold, take these keys and fetch more spices, nurse.

Nurse.   They call for dates and quinces in the pastry.

[Enter old Capulet]

Capulet.   Come, stir, stir, stir! The second cock hath crowed,
The curfew bell hath rung, 'tis three o'clock.
Look to the baked meats, good Angelica;
Spare not for cost.

Nurse.   Go, you cotquean, go,
Get you to bed! Faith, you'll be sick tomorrow
For this night's watching.

Capulet.   No, not a whit. What, I have watched ere now
All night for lesser cause, and ne'er been sick.

Lady Capulet.   Ay, you have been a mouse hunt in your time;
But I will watch you from such watching now.

[Exit Lady and Nurse]

Capulet. A jealous hood, a jealous hood!
          [*Enter three or four Fellows*
          with spits, logs and baskets]

                              Now, fellow,
          What is there?
First Fellow. Things for the cook, sir; but I know not what.
Capulet. Make haste, make haste.
          [*Exit first Fellow*]
          Sirrah, fetch drier logs.
          Call Peter; he will show thee where they are.
Second Fellow. I have a head, sir, that will find out logs
          And never trouble Peter for the matter.
Capulet. Mass, and well said; a merry whoreson, ha!
          Thou shalt be loggerhead.
          [*Exit second Fellow, with the others*]
                              Good faith, 'tis day.
          The County will be here with music straight,
          For so he said he would.
          [*Play music*]
                              I hear him near.
          Nurse! Wife! What, ho! What, nurse, I say!

[*Enter Nurse*]

Go waken Juliet; go and trim her up.
I'll go and chat with Paris. Hie, make haste,
Make haste! The bridegroom he is come already:
Make haste, I say.

[*Exit*]

SCENE V
JULIET'S CHAMBER

Nurse. Mistress! What, mistress! Juliet! Fast, I warrant her, she.
Why, lamb! Why, lady! Fie, you slugabed.
Why, love, I say! Madam; Sweetheart! Why, bride!
What, not a word? You take your pennyworths now;
Sleep for a week; for the next night, I warrant,
The County Paris hath set up his rest
That you shall rest but little. God forgive me!
Marry, and amen. How sound is she asleep!
I needs must wake her. Madam, madam, madam!
Ay, let the County take you in your bed;
He'll fright you up, i' faith. Will it not be?
      [*Draws aside the curtains*]
What, dressed, and in your clothes, and down again?
I must needs wake you. Lady! Lady! Lady!
Alas, alas! Help, help! My lady's dead!
O weraday that ever I was born!
Some *aqua vitae,* ho! My lord! My lady!

[*Enter Mother*]

Lady Capulet. What noise is here?

Nurse.   O lamentable day!

Lady Capulet. What is the matter?

Nurse.   Look, look! O heavy day!

Lady Capulet. O me, O me My child, my only life!
Revive, look up, or I will die with thee!
Help, help! Call help.

[*Enter Father*]

Capulet. For shame, bring Juliet forth; her lord is come.

Nurse. She's dead, deceased; she's dead, alack the day!

Lady Capulet. Alack the day, she's dead, she's dead, she's dead!

Capulet. Ha! Let me see her. Out alas! She's cold,
Her blood is settled, and her joints are stiff;
Life and these lips have long been separated.
Death lies on her like an untimely frost
Upon the sweetest flower of all the field.

Nurse. O lamentable day!

Lady Capulet.   O woeful time!

Capulet.	Death, that hath ta'en her hence to make me wail,
	Ties up my tongue and will not let me speak.
	[*Enter Friar Lawrence and the*
	County Paris, with Musicians]
Friar.	Come, is the bride ready to go to church?
Capulet.	Ready to go, but never to return.
	O son, the night before thy wedding day
	Hath Death lain with thy wife. There she lies,
	Flower as she was, deflowerèd by him.
	Death is my son-in-law, Death is my heir;
	My daughter he hath wedded. I will die
	And leave him all. Life, living, all is Death's.
Paris.	Have I thought, love, to see this morning's face,
	And doth it give me such a sight as this?
Lady Capulet.	Accursed, unhappy, wretched, hateful day!
	Most miserable hour that e'er time saw
	In lasting labor of his pilgrimage!
	But one, poor one, one poor and loving child,
	But one thing to rejoice and solace in,
	And cruel Death hath catched it from my sight.

Nurse. O woe! O woeful, woeful, woeful day!
Most lamentable day, most woeful day
That ever ever I did yet behold!
O day, O day, O day! O hateful day!
Never was seen so black a day as this.
O woeful day! O woeful day!

Paris. Beguiled, divorcèd, wrongèd, spited, slain!
Most detestable Death, by thee beguiled,
By cruel, cruel thee quite overthrown.
O love! O life!—not life, but love in death!

Capulet. Despised, distressèd, hated, martyred, killed!
Uncomfortable time, why cam'st thou now
To murder, murder our solemnity?
O child, O child! My soul, and not my child!
Dead art thou—alack, my child is dead,
And with my child my joys are burièd!

Friar. Peace, ho, for shame! Confusion's cure lives not
In these confusions. Heaven and yourself
Had part in this fair maid—now heaven hath all,
And all the better is it for the maid.
Your part in her you could not keep from death,
But heaven keeps his part in eternal life.

FRIAR LAWRENCE

The most you sought was her promotion,
For 'twas your heaven she should be advanced;
And weep ye now, seeing she is advanced
Above the clouds, as high as heaven itself?
O, in this love, you love your child so ill
That you run mad, seeing that she is well.
She's not well married that lives married long,
But she's best married that dies married young.
Dry up your tears and stick your rosemary
On this fair corse, and, as the custom is,
And in her best array bear her to church;
For though fond nature bids us all lament,
Yet nature's tears are reason's merriment.

Capulet. All things that we ordainèd festival
Turn from their office to black funeral—
Our instruments to melancholy bells,
Our wedding cheer to a sad burial feast;
Our solemn hymns to sullen dirges change;
Our bridal flowers serve for a buried corse;
And all things change them to the contrary.

Friar.   Sir, go you in; and, madam, go with him;

And go, Sir Paris. Everyone prepare

To follow this fair corse unto her grave.

The heavens do low'r upon you for some ill;

Move them no more by crossing their high will.

> [*Exeunt, casting rosemary on*
> *her and shutting the curtains.*
> *Manet Nurse with Musicians*]

First Musician.   Faith, we may put up our pipes and be gone.

Nurse.   Honest good fellows, ah, put up, put up!

For well you know this is a pitiful case.

> [*Exit*]

First Musician.   Ay, by my troth, the case may be amended.

> [*Enter Peter*]

Peter.   Musicians, O, musicians, ''Heart's ease,''

''Heart's ease''! O, and you will have me live,

play ''Heart's ease.''

First Musician.   Why ''Heart's ease''?

Peter. O, musicians, because my heart itself plays "My heart is full." O, play me some merry dump to comfort me.

First Musician. Not a dump we! 'Tis no time to play now.

Peter. You will not then?

First Musician. No.

Peter. I will then give it you soundly.

First Musician. What will you give us?

Peter. No money, on my faith, but the gleek. I will give you the minstrel.

First Musician. Then will I give you the serving-creature.

Peter. Then will I lay the serving-creature's dagger on your pate. I will carry no crotchets. I'll *re* you, I'll *fa* you. Do you note me?

First Musician. And you *re* us and *fa* us, you note us.

Second Musician. Pray you put up your dagger, and put out your wit. Then have at you with my wit!

Peter.	I will dry-beat you with an iron wit, and put up my iron dagger. Answer me like men.

"When griping grief the heart doth wound,
    And doleful dumps the mind oppress,
    Then music with her silver sound"—

Why "silver sound"? Why "music with her silver sound"? What say you, Simon Catling?

First Musician. Marry, sir, because silver hath a sweet sound.

Peter. Pretty! What say you, Hugh Rebeck?

Second Musician. I say "silver sound" because musicians sound for silver.

Peter. Pretty too! What say you, James Soundpost?

Third Musician. Faith, I know not what to say.

Peter. O, I cry you mercy, you are the singer. I will say for you. It is "music with her silver sound" because musicians have no gold for sounding.

"Then music with her silver sound
    With speedy help doth lend redress."
    [*Exit*]

First Musician. What a pestilent knave is this same!

Second Musician. Hang him, Jack! Come, we'll in here, tarry for the mourners, and stay dinner.

[*Exit with others*]

ACT FIVE

CAPULET

SCENE I
MANTUA. A STREET

[Enter Romeo]

Romeo. If I may trust the flattering truth of sleep,

My dreams presage some joyful news at hand.

My bosom's lord sits lightly in his throne,

And all this day an unaccustomed spirit

Lifts me above the ground with cheerful thoughts.

I dreamt my lady came and found me dead

(Strange dream that gives a dead man leave to think!)

And breathed such life with kisses in my lips

That I revived and was an emperor.

Ah me! How sweet is love itself possessed,

When but love's shadows are so rich in joy!

[Enter Romeo's Man Balthasar, booted]

News from Verona! How now, Balthasar?

Dost thou not bring me letters from the friar?

How doth my lady? Is my father well?

How fares my Juliet? That I ask again,

For nothing can be ill if she be well.

Man.	Then she is well, and nothing can be ill.
	Her body sleeps in Capel's monument,
	And her immortal part with angels lives.
	I saw her laid low in her kindred's vault
	And presently took post to tell it you.
	O, pardon me for bringing these ill news,
	Since you did leave it for my office, sir.
Romeo.	Is it e'en so? Then I defy you, stars!
	Thou knowest my lodging. Get me ink and paper
	And hire post horses. I will hence tonight.
Man.	I do beseech you, sir, have patience.
	Your looks are pale and wild and do import
	Some misadventure.
Romeo.	Tush, thou art deceived.
	Leave me and do the thing I bid thee do.
	Hast thou no letters to me from the friar?
Man.	No, my good lord.
Romeo.	No matter. Get thee gone.
	And hire those horses. I'll be with thee straight.
	[*Exit Balthasar*]
	Well, Juliet, I will lie with thee tonight.
	Let's see for means. O mischief, thou art swift
	To enter in the thoughts of desperate men!

I do remember an apothecary,
And hereabouts 'a dwells, which late I noted
In tatt'red weeds, with overwhelming brows,
Culling of simples. Meager were his looks,
Sharp misery had worn him to the bones;
And in his needy shop a tortoise hung,
An alligator stuffed, and other skins
Of ill-shaped fishes; and about his shelves
A beggarly account of empty boxes,
Green earthen pots, bladders, and musty seeds,
Remnants of packthread, and old cakes of roses
Were thinly scatterèd, to make up a show.
Noting this penury, to myself I said,
"And if a man did need a poison now
Whose sale is present death in Mantua,
Here lives a caitiff wretch would sell it him."
O, this same thought did but forerun my need,
And this same needy man must sell it me.
As I remember, this should be the house.
Being holiday, the beggar's shop is shut.
What, ho! Apothecary!
    [*Enter Apothecary*]

Apothecary.	Who calls so loud?
Romeo.	Come hither, man. I see that thou art poor.
	Hold, there is forty ducats. Let me have
	A dram of poison, such soon-speeding gear
	As will disperse itself through all the veins
	That the life-weary taker may fall dead,
	And that the trunk may be discharged of breath
	As violently as hasty powder fired
	Doth hurry from the fatal cannon's womb.
Apothecary.	Such mortal drugs I have; but Mantua's law
	Is death to any he that utters them.
Romeo.	Art thou so bare and full of wretchedness
	And fearest to die? Famine is in thy cheeks,
	Need and oppression starveth in thy eyes,
	Contempt and beggary hangs upon thy back:
	The world is not thy friend, nor the world's law;
	The world affords no law to make thee rich;
	Then be not poor, but break it and take this.
Apothecary.	My poverty but not my will consents.
Romeo.	I pay thy poverty and not thy will.
Apothecary.	Put this in any liquid thing you will
	And drink it off, and if you had the strength
	Of twenty men, it would dispatch you straight.

Romeo. There is thy gold—worse poison to men's souls,
Doing more murder in this loathsome world,
Than these poor compounds that thou mayst not sell.
I sell thee poison; thou hast sold me none.
Farewell. Buy food and get thyself in flesh.
Come, cordial and not poison, go with me
To Juliet's grave; for there must I use thee.
  [*Exeunt*]

SCENE II

FRIAR LAWRENCE'S CELL

[Enter Friar John]

John.   Holy Franciscan friar, brother, ho!

[Enter Friar Lawrence]

Lawrence.   This same should be the voice of Friar John.
    Welcome from Mantua. What says Romeo?
    Or, if his mind be writ, give me his letter.

John.   Going to find a barefoot brother out,
    One of our order, to associate me
    Here in this city visiting the sick,
    And finding him, the searchers of the town,
    Suspecting that we both were in a house
    Where the infectious pestilence did reign,
    Sealed up the doors, and would not let us forth,
    So that my speed to Mantua there was stayed.

Lawrence.   Who bare my letter, then, to Romeo?

John.   I could not send it—here it is again—
    Nor get a messenger to bring it thee,
    So fearful were they of infection.

Lawrence.   Unhappy fortune! By my brotherhood,
The letter was not nice, but full of charge,
Of dear import; and the neglecting it
May do much danger. Friar John, go hence,
Get me an iron crow and bring it straight
Unto my cell.

John.   Brother, I'll go and bring it thee.
        [*Exit*]

Lawrence.   Now must I to the monument alone.
Within this three hours will fair Juliet wake.
She will beshrew me much that Romeo
Hath had no notice of these accidents;
But I will write again to Mantua,
And keep her at my cell till Romeo come—
Poor living corse, closed in a dead man's tomb!
        [*Exit*]

*[Enter Paris and his Page
with flowers, sweet water]*

Paris.   Give me thy torch, boy. Hence, and stand aloof.

Yet put it out, for I would not be seen.

Under yond yew trees lay thee all along,

Holding thy ear close to the hollow ground.

So shall no foot upon the churchyard tread

(Being loose, unfirm, with digging up of graves)

But thou shalt hear it. Whistle then to me,

As signal that thou hearest something approach.

Give me those flowers. Do as I bid thee, go.

Page.   *[Aside]* I am almost afraid to stand alone

Here in the churchyard; yet I will adventure.

       [Retires]

Paris. Sweet flower, with flowers thy bridal bed I strew
(O woe! thy canopy is dust and stones)
Which with sweet water nightly I will dew;
Or, wanting that, with tears distilled by moans.
The obsequies that I for thee will keep
Nightly shall be to strew thy grave and weep.
　　[Whistle Boy]
The boy gives warning something doth approach.
What cursèd foot wanders this way tonight
To cross my obsequies and true love's rite?
What, with a torch? Muffle me, night, awhile.
　　[Retires]
　　[Enter Romeo, and Balthasar with a
　　torch, a mattock, and a crow of iron]

Romeo. Give me that mattock and the wrenching iron.
Hold, take this letter. Early in the morning
See thou deliver it to my lord and father.
Give me the light. Upon thy life I charge thee,
Whate'er thou hearest or seest, stand all aloof
And do not interrupt me in my course.
Why I descend into this bed of death

Is partly to behold my lady's face,
But chiefly to take thence from her dead finger
A precious ring—a ring that I must use
In dear employment. Therefore hence, be gone.
But if thou, jealous, dost return to pry
In what I farther shall intend to do,
By heaven, I will tear thee joint by joint
And strew this hungry churchyard with thy limbs.
The time and my intents are savage-wild,
More fierce and more inexorable far
Than empty tigers or the roaring sea.

Balthasar. I will be gone, sir, and not trouble ye.

Romeo. So shalt thou show me friendship. Take thou that.
Live, and be prosperous; and farewell, good fellow.

Balthasar. [*Aside*] For all this same, I'll hide me hereabout.
His looks I fear, and his intents I doubt.
　　　[*Retires*]

Romeo. Thou detestable maw, thou womb of death,
Gorged with the dearest morsel of the earth,
Thus I enforce thy rotten jaws to open,
And in despite I'll cram thee with more food.
　　　[*Romeo opens the tomb*]

Paris.	This is that banished haughty Montague
	That murd'red my love's cousin—with which grief
	It is supposed the fair creature died—
	And here is come to do some villainous shame
	To the dead bodies. I will apprehend him.
	Stop thy unhallowèd toil, vile Montague!
	Can vengeance be pursued further than death?
	Condemnèd villain, I do apprehend thee.
	Obey, and go with me; for thou must die.
Romeo.	I must indeed; and therefore came I hither.
	Good gentle youth, tempt not a desp'rate man.
	Fly hence and leave me. Think upon these gone;
	Let them affright thee. I beseech thee, youth,
	Put not another sin upon my head
	By urging me to fury. O, be gone!
	By heaven, I love thee better than myself,
	For I come hither armed against myself.
	Stay not, be gone. Live, and hereafter say
	A madman's mercy bid thee run away.
Paris.	I do defy thy conjurations,
	And apprehend thee for a felon here.
Romeo.	Wilt thou provoke me? Then have at thee, boy!
	[*They fight*]

Page.	O Lord, they fight! I will go call the watch.
	[*Exit. Paris falls*]
Paris.	O, I am slain! If thou be merciful,
	Open the tomb, lay me with Juliet.
	[*Dies*]
Romeo.	In faith, I will. Let me peruse this face.
	Mercutio's kinsman, noble County Paris!
	What said my man when my betossèd soul
	Did not attend him as we rode? I think
	He told me Paris should have married Juliet.
	Said he not so, or did I dream it so?
	Or am I mad, hearing him talk of Juliet,
	To think it was so? O, give me thy hand,
	One writ with me in sour misfortune's book!
	I'll bury thee in a triumphant grave.
	A grave? O, no, a lanthorn, slaught'red youth,
	For here lies Juliet, and her beauty makes
	This vault a feasting presence full of light.
	Death, lie thou there, by a dead man interred.
	[*Lays him in the tomb*]
	How oft when men are at the point of death
	Have they been merry! Which their keepers call
	A lightning before death. O, how may I

Call this a lightning? O my love, my wife!
Death, that hath sucked the honey of thy breath,
Hath had no power yet upon thy beauty.
Thou art not conquered. Beauty's ensign yet
Is crimson in thy lips and in thy cheeks,
And death's pale flag is not advancèd there.
Tybalt, liest thou there in thy bloody sheet?
O, what more favor can I do to thee
Than with that hand that cut thy youth in twain
To sunder his that was thine enemy?
Forgive me, cousin! Ah, dear Juliet,
Why art thou yet so fair? Shall I believe
That unsubstantial Death is amorous,
And that the lean abhorrèd monster keeps
Thee here in dark to be his paramour?
For fear of that I still will stay with thee
And never from this pallet of dim night
Depart again. Here, here will I remain
With worms that are thy chambermaids. O, here
Will I set up my everlasting rest
And shake the yoke of inauspicious stars
From this world-wearied flesh. Eyes, look your last!
Arms, take your last embrace! And, lips, O you

The doors of breath, seal with a righteous kiss
A dateless bargain to engrossing death!
Come, bitter conduct; come, unsavory guide!
Thou desperate pilot, now at once run on
The dashing rocks thy seasick weary bark!
Here's to my love!
    [Drinks]
O true apothecary!
Thy drugs are quick. Thus with a kiss I die.
    [Falls]
    [Enter Friar Lawrence, with
    lanthorn and crow and spade]

Friar. Saint Francis be my speed! How oft tonight
Have my old feet stumbled at graves! Who's there?

Balthasar. Here's one, a friend, and one that knows you well.

Friar. Bliss be upon you! Tell me, good my friend,
What torch is yond that vainly lends his light
To grubs and eyeless skulls? As I discern,
It burneth in the Capels' monument.

Balthasar. It doth so, holy sir; and there's my master,
One that you love.

Friar.   Who is it?

Balthasar.   Romeo.

Friar. How long hath he been there?

MONTAGUE

ISADORE SELTZER

Balthasar.	Full half an hour.
Friar.	Go with me to the vault.
Balthasar.	I dare not, sir.

My master knows not but I am gone hence,
And fearfully did menace me with death
If I did stay to look on his intents.

Friar. Stay then; I'll go alone. Fear comes upon me.
O, much I fear some ill unthrifty thing.

Balthasar. As I did sleep under this yew tree here,
I dreamt my master and another fought,
And that my master slew him.

Friar. Romeo!
Alack, alack, what blood is this which stains
The stony entrance of this sepulcher?
What mean these masterless and gory swords
To lie discolored by this place of peace?
[*Enters the tomb*]
Romeo! O, pale! Who else? What, Paris too?
And steeped in blood? Ah, what an unkind hour
Is guilty of this lamentable chance!
The lady stirs.
[*Juliet rises*]

Juliet.	O comfortable friar! Where is my lord?
	I do remember well where I should be,
	And there I am. Where is my Romeo?
Friar.	I hear some noise. Lady, come from that nest
	Of death, contagion, and unnatural sleep.
	A greater power than we can contradict
	Hath thwarted our intents. Come, come away.
	Thy husband in thy bosom there lies dead;
	And Paris too. Come, I'll dispose of thee
	Among a sisterhood of holy nuns.
	Stay not to question, for the watch is coming.
	Come, go, good Juliet. I dare no longer stay.
Juliet.	Go, get thee hence, for I will not away.
	[*Exit Friar*]
	What's here? A cup, closed in my truelove's hand?
	Poison, I see, hath been his timeless end.
	O churl! Drunk all, and left no friendly drop
	To help me after? I will kiss thy lips.
	Haply some poison yet doth hang on them
	To make me die with a restorative.
	[*Kisses him*]
	Thy lips are warm!

Chief Watchman.	[*Within*] Lead, boy. Which way?
Juliet.	Yea, noise? Then I'll be brief. O happy dagger!
	[*Snatches Romeo's dagger*]
	This is thy sheath; there rust, and let me die.
	[*She stabs herself and falls*]
	[*Enter Paris' Boy and Watch*]
Boy.	This is the place. There, where the torch doth burn.
Chief Watchman.	The ground is bloody. Search about the churchyard.
	Go, some of you; whoe'er you find attach.
	[*Exeunt some of the Watch*]
	Pitiful sight! Here lies the County slain;
	And Juliet bleeding, warm, and newly dead,
	Who here hath lain this two days burièd.
	Go, tell the Prince; run to the Capulets;
	Raise up the Montagues; some others search.
	[*Exeunt others of the Watch*]
	We see the ground whereon these woes do lie,
	But the true ground of all these piteous woes
	We cannot without circumstance descry.
	[*Enter several of the Watch,*
	with Romeo's man Balthasar]
Second Watchman.	Here's Romeo's man. We found him in the churchyard.

Chief Watchman. Hold him in safety till the Prince come hither.
[*Enter Friar Lawrence and another Watchman*]

Third Watchman. Here is a friar that trembles, sighs, and weeps.
We took this mattock and this spade from him
As he was coming from this churchyard's side.

Chief Watchman. A great suspicion! Stay the friar too.
[*Enter the Prince and Attendants*]

Prince. What misadventure is so early up,
That calls our person from our morning rest?
[*Enter Capulet and his Wife with others*]

Capulet. What should it be, that is so shrieked abroad?

Lady Capulet. O, the people in the street cry "Romeo,"
Some "Juliet," and some "Paris"; and all run
With open outcry toward our monument.

Prince. What fear is this which startles in your ears?

Chief Watchman. Sovereign, here lies the County Paris slain;
And Romeo dead; and Juliet, dead before,
Warm and new killed.

Prince. Search, seek, and know how this foul murder comes.

Chief Watchman. Here is a friar, and slaughtered Romeo's man,
With instruments upon them fit to open
These dead men's tombs.

Capulet.	O heavens! O wife, look how our daughter bleeds!
	This dagger hath mista'en, for, lo, his house
	Is empty on the back of Montague,
	And it missheathèd in my daughter's bosom!
Lady Capulet.	O me, this sight of death is as a bell
	That warns my old age to a sepulcher.

[*Enter Montague and others*]

Prince.	Come, Montague; for thou art early up
	To see thy son and heir more early down.
Montague.	Alas, my liege, my wife is dead tonight!
	Grief of my son's exile hath stopped her breath.
	What further woe conspires against mine age?
Prince.	Look, and thou shalt see.
Montague.	O thou untaught! What manners is in this,
	To press before thy father to a grave?
Prince.	Seal up the mouth of outrage for a while,
	Till we can clear these ambiguities
	And know their spring, their head, their true descent;
	And then will I be general of your woes
	And lead you even to death. Meantime forbear,
	And let mischance be slave to patience.
	Bring forth the parties of suspicion.

Friar.	I am the greatest, able to do least,
	Yet most suspected, as the time and place
	Doth make against me, of this direful murder;
	And here I stand, both to impeach and purge
	Myself condemnèd and myself excused.
Prince.	Then say at once what thou dost know in this.
Friar.	I will be brief, for my short date of breath
	Is not so long as is a tedious tale.
	Romeo, there dead, was husband to that Juliet;
	And she, there dead, that's Romeo's faithful wife.
	I married them; and their stol'n marriage day
	Was Tybalt's doomsday, whose untimely death
	Banished the new-made bridegroom from this city;
	For whom, and not for Tybalt, Juliet pined.
	You, to remove that siege of grief from her,
	Betrothed and would have married her perforce
	To County Paris. Then comes she to me
	And with wild looks bid me devise some mean
	To rid her from this second marriage,
	Or in my cell there would she kill herself.
	Then gave I her (so tutored by my art)
	A sleeping potion; which so took effect

As I intended, for it wrought on her
The form of death. Meantime I writ to Romeo
That he should hither come as this dire night
To help to take her from her borrowed grave,
Being the time the potion's force should cease.
But he which bore my letter, Friar John,
Was stayed by accident, and yesternight
Returned my letter back. Then all alone
At the prefixèd hour of her waking
Came I to take her from her kindred's vault;
Meaning to keep her closely at my cell
Till I conveniently could send to Romeo.
But when I came, some minute ere the time
Of her awakening, here untimely lay
The noble Paris and true Romeo dead.
She wakes; and I entreated her come forth
And bear this work of heaven with patience;
But then a noise did scare me from the tomb,
And she, too desperate, would not go with me,
But, as it seems, did violence on herself.
All this I know, and to the marriage
Her nurse is privy; and if aught in this

Miscarried by my fault, let my old life
Be sacrificed some hour before his time
Unto the rigor of severest law.

Prince. We still have known thee for a holy man.
Where's Romeo's man? What can he say to this?

Balthasar. I brought my master news of Juliet's death;
And then in post he came from Mantua
To this same place, to this same monument.
This letter he early bid me give his father,
And threat'ned me with death, going in the vault,
If I departed not and left him there.

Prince. Give me the letter. I will look on it.
Where is the County's page that raised the watch?
Sirrah, what made your master in this place?

Boy. He came with flowers to strew his lady's grave;
And bid me stand aloof, and so I did.
Anon comes one with light to ope the tomb;
And by and by my master drew on him;
And then I ran away to call the watch.

Prince. This letter doth make good the friar's words,
Their course of love, the tidings of her death;
And here he writes that he did buy a poison
Of a poor pothecary and therewithal
Came to this vault to die and lie with Juliet.
Where be these enemies? Capulet, Montague,
See what a scourge is laid upon your hate,
That heaven finds means to kill your joys with love.
And I, for winking at your discords too,
Have lost a brace of kinsmen. All are punished.

Capulet. O brother Montague, give me thy hand.
This is my daughter's jointure, for no more
Can I demand.

Montague.   But I can give thee more;
For I will raise her statue in pure gold,
That whiles Verona by that name is known,
There shall no figure at such rate be set
As that of true and faithful Juliet.

Capulet. As rich shall Romeo's by his lady's lie—
Poor sacrifices of our enmity!

Prince. A glooming peace this morning with it brings.
The sun for sorrow will not show his head.
Go hence, to have more talk of these sad things;
Some shall be pardoned, and some punishèd;
For never was a story of more woe
Than this of Juliet and her Romeo.

[*Exeunt omnes*]

FINIS

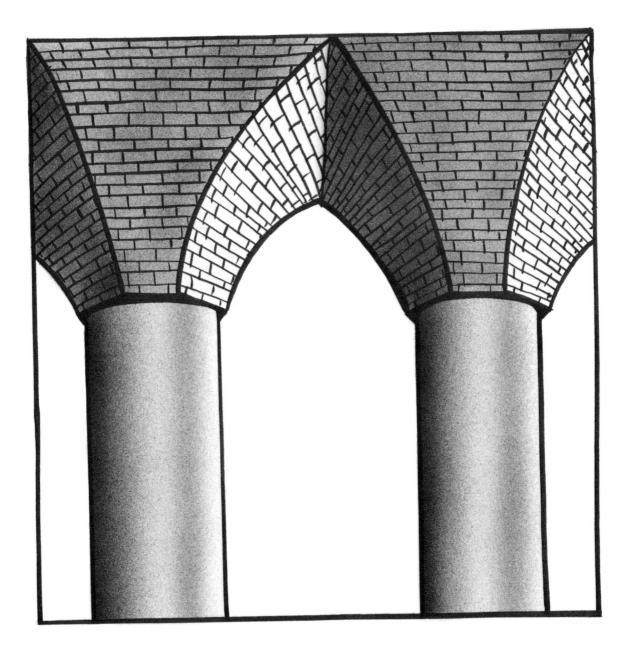

COLOPHON

Typography by Royal Composing Room, Inc.
The text is set in 14 pt. Cloister Bold with 12 pt. Italics.
All display copy is Photo Display Cloister and Cloister Bold.
Complete page negatives, ready for platemaking were prepared.
Printed lithography by Rae Publishing Co., Inc.
The paper, manufactured by Finch, Pruyn & Company, Inc.,
is Finch Opaque, Vellum Finish, Bright White, Basis 80.
Binding by A. Horowitz & Son/Bookbinders, with Kingston
Natural Cloth and Black Permacote Skytogen Embossed
for the slipcase. Endpapers are Elephant Hide Royal Blue.
Typographic coordination by Irving Levine.
Illustrations by Isadore Seltzer.
Design by Daniel Haberman.

WILLIAM SHAKESPEARE:
THE TRAGEDY OF ROMEO AND JULIET